With no remaining family, and the remnants of a relationship gone wrong, thirty-one-year-old Essie moves from the city to a small Wisconsin town after inheriting her late nana's Victorian home. Essie hopes for a fresh start, but little does she know what secrets the house contains and the many lives and difficult decisions the new town will put in her path. Through two small boys, Essie meets two men who will play a big part in her life.

First, there's Pete, the mysterious man of many talents who befriends her and with whom she feels so at ease. No one knows who he is, where he came from, or why he chose this small town to settle in. Could he be befriending her in a scheme to get his hands on her nana's property?

Then there's Lark, the handsome schoolteacher who seems to keep finding a way into Essie's life. Essie's falling for him, but will his involvement with Diana prevent her from opening her heart back up to another chance at finding love?

And Two Makes Four
Copyright © 2023 Audrey Dean
ISBN: 978-1-4874-3725-1
Cover art by Tyffani Lyons

Published by eXtasy Books Inc

Look for us online at:
www.eXtasybooks.com

AND TWO MAKES FOUR

BY

AUDREY DEAN

DEDICATION

To my granddaughter, Stephany, who spent endless hours helping me with my computer, and to my granddaughter, Arianne, for her editing and finetuning of the story. Without their patience and help, this would not have been possible.

CHAPTER ONE

As Essie rounded the corner, she saw her grandmother's house standing in disarray, the paint peeling, the shutters hanging askew. To her surprise, although the lawn grew long and shaggy, it wasn't the tangled and weedy mess she expected for a lawn unattended for two years. Who is the good Samaritan? she wondered.

She got out of the car and stretched her legs, tired from the long ride. As she searched for the key she'd carried with her the two years since her nana's funeral, an overwhelming sense of nostalgia caused a lump to form in her throat. Her heart leaped with anticipation as she unlocked the door to the house. At that time, Essie realized nothing was the same as her young imagination remembered it. *Has it really been twenty-one years?*

In the mind of a ten-year-old child, she'd played right there in a beautiful courtyard surrounding a magnificent castle with its big pillars rising as high as her imagination could take her. She remembered the huge front door with its shiny gold handles, opening into a grand entrance with high ceilings, beautiful mirrors, and pictures of stately-looking gentlemen plastered along the walls. Her problems momentarily left her, and her lips curled into a smile as she recalled the names her young imagination had labeled the pictures. King George, Sir Galahad, Prince Sammie. The home of her fairy godmother — her nana — where the family had visited twice a year, once in the summer and again at Christmas, now belonged to her. Empty since her nana died, she'd stayed away, battling

1

against her feelings of guilt and unworthiness for two long years. But now, she had nowhere else to go.

Essie looked around, feeling lost in memories of the last time she'd been to the house. Out of all the rooms, the parlor was her favorite. Surrounded by so many of her nana's things, she could almost feel her nearby. With its big bay window, the octagon-shaped room overlooked the front rose garden that snuggled up against the house. In the center of the room, almost like a throne waiting for its queen, accompanied by a small side table, sat her nana's favorite rocking chair. The wallpaper was faded and torn in several places. The drapes hung old and dusty. It was here in this room that she had the most vivid memories of her nana.

Her last time here, Brad had been with her, not because he wanted to be, but because she'd somehow convinced him to come to her nana's funeral. In their three years together, Brad, with his enchanting eyes and remarkable good looks, had managed to completely destroy her dream fantasy. She felt determined to reclaim the hope that had been stolen from her. She wouldn't waste her time regretting the past. In this sleepy little town of Rosepoint, nestled in the heart of Wisconsin, she'd determined to somehow pull herself together and start all over again. She would get a good night's sleep because tomorrow would be the first day of a new beginning for her. She put on her pajamas and snuggled in the same bed where so many of her dreams had started.

Essie woke to a thump, thump, thump coming from somewhere outside.

Out of habit, her eyes scanned the clock on her bedside stand. She threw back the covers and jumped to the floor. Tension eased, and her shoulders relaxed as she surveyed her surroundings and remembered she had no schedule to keep. She got up, put on her robe, and went to look out the kitchen window, rubbing her bleary eyes with the back of her hand. A bright stream of sunlight shining through the debris on the dirty window formed small shadows on the countertop that danced around as the fluttering leaves of the tall maple tree blew in the wind.

A small boy, about seven years old, stood there bouncing a large rubber ball on a cement slab in front of a shabby little shed in the backyard. Essie was fascinated by his fiery red hair and the intensity with which he concentrated on what he did. She opened the door and stepped out onto the small wooden porch. A nip in the air introduced her to Wisconsin's chilly fall season.

"Good morning," she called out softly, trying not to startle the boy.

The boy spun around, catching himself on the side of the shed.

"Morning. Who are you?"

"I'm Essie. I live here. This is my house." She walked to the edge of the porch.

"I thought this was Mr. Pete's house. Nobody's ever been living here before."

She could see the baffled look on his face. "Who's Mr. Pete?"

"He's my friend. He told me I could have my secret club-house here if I didn't bother anything." He pointed to the small shed behind him.

"And do you? Bother anything, I mean?"

"Sometimes I peek in the window, just to see if I can see what's inside, but I don't bother nothing." He tipped his head and squinted up at her.

"Where does this Mr. Pete live?"

"He lives by Mr. Johnson. He mows the grass. Sometimes I help him rake it up. He gives me a dollar if I do a good job." He held the ball under his arm, nervously rubbing its squeaky surface and looking sideways at her.

Essie felt more of the pent-up anxiety leave her, and her whole body relaxed as she talked to this adorable little intruder. "And this secret club . . . I suppose you have lots of members."

He giggled. "No, how could I? It's a secret. Besides, Mr. Pete said I could only have my friend, Joey, if we would be good and not tell anybody else."

With her curiosity piqued, she questioned who this Mr. Pete was to take authority over her nana's house. "That sounds like a good idea. You didn't tell me your name."

"It's Jamie." He bounced the ball, then threw it against the wall and jumped to the side to catch it.

"Jamie. I like that name. And where do you live, Jamie?" She stepped closer to him.

"I live with my grandma. You know, Miss Ida Belle."

"Miss Ida Belle?"

Jamie giggled. "Everybody knows Miss Ida Belle." He tipped his head to the side.

"But I'm new here. Tell me why everyone knows her." She smiled at his childlike innocence.

"Cause she's lived hundreds of years, and she knows everybody who's ever been born here."

Essie chuckled. "And your friend, Joey, tell me about him. I bet you do lots of things together."

"Yeah! Sometimes Mr. Pete and Mr. Winters take us fishing."

"That sounds like fun. Who's Mr. Winters?"

"That's Joey's daddy. He's my teacher." Jamie opened the shed door and threw the ball inside.

"Well, Jamie, as long as you and Joey don't tell any other kids about your secret club, you can keep coming here. You'll have to keep the same rules as Mr. Pete made, though. Do not bother anything, but no more peeking in the windows, okay?"

"Okay. I have to go tell Mr. Pete somebody's living in his house." Jamie took off running through the tall grass, his red hair flying in the breeze.

Essie grinned to herself at the sight of the small boy speeding off as fast as he could, his jacket literally standing out behind him.

She stepped down from the porch to the small shed. In one corner, an old stuffed chair with a broken arm was shoved back against the wall. In front of it sat a wooden crate. Over against the other wall was a large cardboard box turned upside down and covered with what looked like an old curtain, squatted with age and about ready to fall. Above it, on the wall, hung a small chalkboard. Printed on it in large letters read, *The J Club.*

"Of course," she said to herself, "Jamie and Joey." She breathed in a big breath of the fresh, crisp air and marveled at her peaceful surroundings. Always fond of children, her mother had encouraged her to be a teacher, but her memory of her fifth-grade teacher, Miss Heartman—called her Miss Heartless—had discouraged her to do so. In her junior and senior years, she did volunteer work at an after-school children's center in Tulsa just to be around children.

She couldn't think of a better way to start her day. Visions of her nana and their tea parties made her feel all warm inside. Nana would pour milk into Essie's cup, put a little coffee in it to make it colored, and sit with her for hours pretending to be her fairy godmother. What she needed now was the real stuff.

She went inside, found her nana's coffee pot, measured four spoons of coffee, and filled it with water. When it was ready, she walked around the various rooms of the house, sipping her coffee and mulling over memories. Each bedroom, with its fluffy bedspreads and frilly curtains, reminded her of the times Nana cuddled with her and read Essie's favorite *Cinderella* story.

She went to the bookcase in the hallway, her eyes searching for the familiar cover. She found it there, along with several other of her favorites, stuffed into the shelf, dusty and smelly, their pages yellowed and crisp with age. She picked it up and opened the cover. Fingering through it, a wave of nostalgia swept over her as she saw the childlike scribbles made so many years ago.

Sitting close by, stood the picture of her nana holding her as a baby. She squeezed her eyes tightly together, trying to stop the tears, but she was unsuccessful at putting the memories out of her mind. She put the book gently back in its place and went into her bedroom.

As she finished dressing, she jumped at the sound of the doorbell. Swallowing the last sip of her coffee, she went downstairs to answer. Jamie stood there, a proud grin on his face as if to say he'd brought his most prized possession. Beside him, in jeans and a tan, wrinkled shirt, stood a man with thinning brown hair and blue eyes, probably in his early to mid-forties, but he had an air about him she couldn't decipher. His skin was tanned, his brow furrowed, and he had that weathered look. This led her to believe his life had not been easy, yet the twinkle in his eye and the ease with which he stood there drew her to him immediately.

He stuck his hand out to greet her. "Hi, Peter Thornton."

"Mr. Pete." She grinned as she reached out to greet him.

Pete tousled Jamie's hair. "One and the same," he said.

"I'm Essie Euller. Please come in." She gestured to the sofa.

"Miss Tessie's granddaughter?" he asked, sitting on the sofa and motioning for Jamie to sit beside him.

Essie's head snapped to attention. "You were a friend of my grandmother?"

Pete shook his head. "No, I've only been here in Rosepoint for about a year and a half. This is a small town. But word gets around. We knew you would be coming sooner or later."

"So tell me, Mr. Pete, how did it come about that you've been mowing my grass? By the way, I want to thank you for that."

He shrugged his shoulders. "I had the time, and it needed cutting. And please, call me Pete."

"It would have been a real mess. I really appreciate it."

"I wanted to come here and explain about the old shed out back. It sat empty, and no one knew you would be coming so soon, so I acted beyond my authority and gave the boys permission to use it. I'm sorry, but they're good boys, and Joey's dad and I have kept a close eye on them. They haven't bothered anything."

Essie winked at Jamie. "Except maybe peeking in the windows."

Jamie blushed, stuck his tongue in his cheek, and looked slyly at Mr. Pete.

"I've already told Jamie they could keep their secret clubhouse," Essie said. "Of course, since I know all about it, I guess that makes me a member. Otherwise, it wouldn't be a secret club."

Pete bent toward Jamie and looked the boy directly in the eyes. "Do you hear that, Jamie? I think you should thank Miss Essie, don't you?"

Jamie nodded shyly.

"But only if you let me be the officer in charge of cookies and lemonade." Essie reached out and took Jamie's hand in a big shake. "Now, when do I get to meet the other member of our secret club?"

Jamie shrugged his shoulders. "Probably after church tomorrow."

Pete stood and put his arm around Jamie's shoulder. "I think we've taken enough of Miss Essie's time. Miss Ida is probably wondering where you are."

"So nice to meet you, Mr. Pete, and I'll see you soon,

Jamie." Essie held her breath, smothering the giggle trying to force its way out. The twinkle in Mr. Pete's eye told her they would become great friends. She stepped away from the door with a feeling of peace in her heart. Yes, sir, she was going to be just fine here in her nana's house.

On that bright Sunday morning, after a good night's sleep, Essie hummed a soft tune while she sat under the big maple tree in her backyard. While she sat basking in its rays, the sunshine found its way through the occasional opening in the big tree to give her the warmth she needed. She listened to the soothing chatter of the robins as they voiced their objection to the presence of the tiny, but vicious hummingbirds. A good cup of coffee, her favorite time of the day, and a new hope for the future had her in a good mood. Only a couple of days here, and already she'd made two new friends. There was Jamie, the cute little red-headed boy, so full of animation that he reminded her of a *Disney* character, and his mysterious sidekick, Mr. Pete, who went around mowing people's grass just because it needed mowing.

Contemplating the rest of her day, Essie decided to go for a walk around the neighborhood. Not surprised to see that it was an older neighborhood with larger homes, well-kept lawns, and pretty flowers, she strolled along, enjoying the crisp fresh air. She passed one lady sitting on her porch and received a friendly wave.

In another yard, a little girl and her dog chased a soccer ball. *What a beautiful day for a walk, and what a perfect neighborhood.* Just as she rounded the corner of her block on the way back, a black pickup truck pulled up in front of her house. A man and a small boy got out and walked toward her front door.

Speeding up her steps, she called out, "Hello, I'm Essie Euller. May I help you?" The man turned at the sound of her voice. No doubt the other half of the *J Club* and his father had come to call. Essie thought the man certainly had the look of a self-confident teacher.

"I'm Lark Winters, and this is my son." Lark extended his hand and gave her a firm shake.

"Let me guess, Joey?" Essie interrupted.

The towheaded little boy with freckles scattered across his nose, and one front tooth missing, grinned up at his dad, and they all laughed.

"Well, it's nice to meet you both. I guess you know I met your buddy Jamie and Mr. Pete yesterday," she said, speaking to Joey.

"And I have an idea you'll be meeting a lot more of the townspeople in the next few days," Lark said. "This is a very friendly little community. Just a little warning, though. Pete announced at church that we have a new neighbor in town." He shook his head and chuckled. "You'll be deluged with ladies bringing cookies and cakes and freshly baked breads. I came by to welcome you without the cake and cookies, though. I'm not very handy in the kitchen, I'm afraid."

"Oh my." She patted her stomach. "I don't need any help from the friendly neighbors, but it does sound delicious. I'm really looking forward to meeting everyone."

"We're mostly just one big family here. I'm sure you'll fit right in," Lark assured her.

"Did you know my grandmother?" She raised her brow as she waited for his answer.

"Yes, I met Miss Tessie at some of our school functions. I'm a teacher over at the elementary school. I've been in town for about six years."

"So you aren't a native either?" she inquired.

"No, but it won't take long for you to feel like one." Lark put his hands in his pocket and smiled at her. "Maybe two weeks! This town can pull you into the center of things faster than anywhere I've ever lived."

Essie's heart skipped a beat. Was she ready to embrace a whole town? Her mind had been in such a state of confusion when she left Tulsa that the only thought she had was one of solitude. She'd already begun to see that may not be a possibility in Rosepoint.

"I hear you and Pete have been keeping an eye on my place for me. I really appreciate it."

"We all miss Miss Tessie. It would be a shame to let anything happen to this place." He gestured toward her house. "The stately old homes like this are what makes our town so quaint."

Essie laughed. "I'm afraid this stately old house is in great need of repairs. I plan on putting it back in order, but it'll take a while."

"It sounds like you plan on sticking around."

"I hope so. I can't wait for all those cakes and breads to show up at my door." She patted her stomach again.

Lark chuckled. "If you need any help getting rid of them, let me know."

"You and your whole family are invited." She laughed back.

"It's only the two of us," Lark said, ruffling Joey's hair. "But he can do pretty good when it comes to cake and cookies, huh, Bud?" He put his arm fondly around his son's shoulder. "About the old shed . . . we'll find the boys someplace else to play. They don't need to be bothering you."

"I can't take their clubhouse away from them," Essie said, winking at Joey. "Besides, I'm an official member now, or didn't Jamie tell you?"

Lark looked at her. His deep green eyes were aglow. "Sounds like something you got roped into."

"I have no use for the shed. As long as they don't bring a whole gang, I'll enjoy having them around."

"Welcome to our little town." He stepped forward and offered her his hand again. "I know you'll fit right in once you get acquainted. We have lots of activities going on year-round. I hope to see you soon."

"That depends on how soon those cakes show up." Essie blushed at her own boldness. "I'm going to call you. You'll see."

Lark chuckled. "Say goodbye to Miss Essie, Joey."

Slapping herself softly on the side of the face and shaking her head from side to side, Essie watched the two leave. Oh, goodness, had she been flirting with Lark Winters? No, she thought. She'd definitely sworn off any romantic relationship after Brad had shattered her fantasy dream and sent her reeling back into the world of reality. This good-looking teacher, with his dark hair, sparkling green eyes, and intense concentration, must have all the single ladies in Rosepoint competing for his attention.

Monday morning found Essie sprawled on the floor with her nana's personal papers around her, discarding whatever she found she could part with. Fascinated by the bundle of cards she'd found at the bottom of a shoe box, she untied the pink satin ribbon that held them together. Evidently important to her nana, Essie felt warm inside as she sought to unlock every insight into her nana's life. Birthday and Christmas cards, all from Essie to her nana, beginning when she was barely able to print her name, fell to the old, faded carpet. A tear prickled the corner of her eye. Her heart ached as she struggled to push the thought from her mind of not keeping in closer contact with her nana after the death of her parents. She had for a while, but her grief overshadowed all others in her life, and she had to admit she let Brad lead her wherever he wanted in that time of weakness.

The loud rumbling of a lawn mower suddenly interrupted

her thoughts. Pulling herself up from the papers, she went to the window. She stood there and gazed outside, watching as Pete mowed her lawn and raked the long grass clippings into a pile before loading them into a garbage bag. Standing there watching him, she imagined a normal family life for a moment. Bringing her thoughts back to the present, she realized she'd been lost in a fantasy. She knew nothing about Pete, not where he came from, nor what he did for a living. Yet there he stood, giving his time to help someone he hardly knew. She could offer to pay him, or would that insult him? Maybe she should go help him. After all, it was her lawn and her responsibility. She slipped on her shoes, grabbed a pair of work gloves, and went outside.

"I see my good Samaritan neighbor is hard at work," Essie said, holding up her gloves. "I thought the least I could do is come and help you."

Pete greeted her with a grin. "Good morning. I thought I'd better cut this grass before I had to bring in a hay machine. I don't normally let it get this long."

"You know you don't have to do this. I can look for a lawn service or maybe even learn how to do it myself."

"Aw, and take my job away from me? I thought I was doing a pretty good job, and you can't beat the price."

Essie chuckled at the childish pout on Pete's face. "At least let me pay you. A person's time is valuable. I can't expect you to do this for nothing. Otherwise, I'll have to start doing your laundry to repay you."

"I must admit that sounds tempting, but I don't charge for helping out the neighbors. I do it because I want to," he said with conviction.

"I appreciate your generosity, but everyone needs money to survive," she insisted.

"That's true." He nodded as he reached for a bag, unfolding it and loading the leaves. "We'd better get to work. I want to do Miss Ida's lawn yet today."

Another hour passed before they finished mowing the lawn and bagging up the grass clippings for the garbage man to take. Essie removed her gloves and brushed the grass from her hair and clothes.

"I have a fresh pitcher of lemonade made. Would you like a glass?"

"I'd love a glass. Thank you." Pete brushed off an old lawn chair and plopped down in it.

Essie went into the house to get the drinks. When she came out, she smiled as she noticed the other chair had been brushed clean. She handed the glass of lemonade to Pete and sat down. "So, Mr. Pete, what brings you to a little town like Rosepoint? There can't be much going on in the way of jobs."

"No, there isn't."

She waited, but he said no more. "May I ask where you're from?"

He shrugged his shoulders. "Here and there. I guess you could say the world is my home." He quickly changed the subject. "By the way, I'll drop by in a day or so and fix that broken step. I wouldn't want you to fall and get hurt on it."

Essie leaned back in the chair and took a big drink of the lemonade. "I plan on hiring someone to do some of those things when I get settled. I can't ask you to do that."

Pete shot her a look. "You didn't ask. I'm volunteering. It'll only take a couple pieces of lumber and a few nails. It's dangerous the way it is."

She shook her head and smiled. "The all-around handyman. Is there anything you can't do?"

He laughed as he rose and handed her the empty glass. "Put me in the kitchen or on a computer, and I'm lost. Thanks for the lemonade. I need to be going if I'm to get Miss Ida's grass cut before dark."

She stood and walked with him toward the street. "Say hi

to Jamie for me."

"I will. He should be home from school by now. He'll be waiting for me, waiting to earn his dollar. He doesn't know it, but his company is worth much more than a dollar to me."

Essie watched as Pete sauntered off down the street in a leisurely manner. His abrupt answers sparked her curiosity even further.

The next afternoon Jamie and Joey showed up accompanied by Lark. "I just wanted to check again to be sure it's okay for the boys to come over. I don't want them bothering you."

A warmness enveloped Essie, thinking of her two new little friends. "They won't bother me. Are you sure you didn't smell those cookies I just baked?" she asked, a touch of mischief in her voice.

"All the way from the school," Lark answered.

Smiling to herself, Essie went inside and got the cookies and a large pitcher of lemonade for her guests. When she returned with the goodies, the boys took their treats into the clubhouse, and she and Lark sat on the small porch in the back.

"I see Pete must have been over cutting your lawn for you," Lark commented as he settled into one of the old, faded lawn chairs.

"Yes, I appreciate his help, but I can't expect him to do that for me. If I'm going to live here, I need to be responsible for taking care of all these things. I'll have to find someone to hire. Do you know anyone who would do that kind of work?"

"Yep! His name's Pete."

"I mean someone who will let me pay them."

"Good luck in getting rid of Pete." Lark took a long drink of the lemonade and let out a sigh of approval. "He mows for half the town's widows and single ladies. Won't take any money from any of them."

"So I've heard. Does he have a job? I really would like to know something about him." She nibbled on a cookie and continued. "I asked him about himself, but he didn't seem to want to say anything. He sort of shut me off. Wouldn't even tell me where he's from."

He chuckled. "He does that to everybody. He just showed up one day and rented an apartment from Mr. Johnson. Unless he works from home, I don't think he has a job." Lark took another cookie from the plate, a thoughtful look on his face. "He always generously donates when we have a cause here in town, so he must be okay financially. He lives modestly and quietly, not bothering anyone, but he's always one of the first to show up if anyone needs help."

"How did he start to mow my lawn, and how long has he been doing it?" Essie asked.

"It wasn't long after he came. He inquired all around town about the house and who'd lived there, and how long the earlier owner had been dead. Seemed really interested in its history. He wanted to know if it would be okay if he mowed the grass. Since your attorney only had it mowed when it got knee-high, I'm sure everyone thought it was a good idea."

"What do you think of him? He's been just wonderful to me, and I appreciate it, but I certainly don't want to get involved with the wrong type of person."

"Do you mean is it safe to have him around?" Lark grinned. "I believe he's a genuinely nice guy who may have had some hard times in his past. I've never heard one bad word about him, and you can be sure if Miss Ida lets him befriend Jamie, he's been thoroughly checked out."

"One thing I'd like to know is why he's so interested in the history of my grandmother's house? I guess I'm a little wary because I've been taken advantage of so many times." She straightened up and extended her chin forward. "But he better know I'll fight till death to defend my nana's precious house."

What an interesting lady, Lark thought as he and Joey made their way home. He could see she definitely liked children and, funny, with his cautious nature when it came to his students, he felt no reason to be afraid for Joey and Jamie. For a young lady of her age to pull up roots all by herself and move to a strange town and undertake the task of redoing an old mansion, it seemed to him an undertaking most people, especially a young lady, wouldn't do. And her interest in Pete led him to believe she wasn't involved with anyone else. Even though he'd not dated since the loss of his wife, Jane, he felt a small twinge of jealousy.

Chapter Two

A lmost immediately following Pete's announcement at church, Essie started meeting her neighbors. Mrs. Dawson, a sweet motherly type from down the street, Dee Bently, who ran the beauty shop, and Annie Coburn with her astounding gift of gab. Gossip and all, Essie heard the history of the whole town in twenty minutes. Even Jamie's grandmother, Miss Ida Belle, came to visit with her friend Florence Rhienholt. And true to Lark's word, they all brought goodies.

Beyond entertaining her new neighbors, Essie found herself busier than she expected. Making a list, she saw even more repairs to be done around the house than she'd first realized. Her nana had neglected to do even the little things necessary for the upkeep of a house that size. Essie didn't worry about the money for the repairs, so her biggest problem was deciding where to start. Her grandfather had owned the local lumber mill and had left her nana with a comfortable living. As her only living relative, Essie received a sizable inheritance when her nana died. She fully intended to restore the beautiful manor to its original grandeur.

Essie sauntered through the house, taking in the full scope of her daunting renovation project, her mind wandering, as it often did lately, to Lark. Should she really invite him over to share some of the sweets, or would that be too naive? As she thought about it, she had no intention, and certainly no expectations, of pursuing a relationship with the charming schoolteacher. But she couldn't eat all those desserts on her own, so maybe she'd bundle up some of them and send them home with Joey. She could also share with Pete, as she remembered he lacked skills when it came to the kitchen,

When Jamie and Joey came by the next afternoon, Essie let them pick their treat from all the goodies she had on hand. Sitting with them in the clubhouse while they ate and drank their lemonade brought to mind a portion of her childhood fantasy of a perfect family. The only thing lacking was her prince charming.

Awestruck at the sight, her mouth flew open when she noticed the sign. Between J and CLUB, someone had squeezed in an E. She was officially a member of their secret club now. Funny how it made her feel. The simple act of being accepted without judgment into the lives of these two little boys made her realize how deeply she'd been wounded by Brad, and how much she needed other people in her life.

Watching the two boys together brought back a feeling of childlike innocence and carefree existence that had been a huge part of her life growing up. She knew she'd been spoiled, not only by her parents but by her nana, as well. She had so many fond memories of the magical times spent with Nana right here in this house, and it delighted her to know she could make some of those memories come alive for Jamie and Joey.

She got up, went into the house, and carefully arranged an array of deserts on a plate for each of them. Listening as she heard Lark's pickup parking in front of her house, her heart gave a quick beat.

"Stop it," she scolded herself quietly as she handed a plate to each of the boys. "Be careful, okay!"

"Dad!" Joey ran to greet Lark, as the plate of goodies bounced up and down. "Miss Essie sent us all kinds of delicious things to eat." He held the plate out for his dad to take.

Lark unwrapped the foil. "Yum. I see Miss Ida's famous

pecan pie, and that would be Mrs. Dawson's chocolate cake. Did you thank Miss Essie?"

Joey turned back to Essie. "Thank you," he said shyly.

"You're welcome, but I hope they're all still in one piece." She ruffled Joey's hair. "Kind of forgot to carry them carefully, huh?"

"No problem. One of my favorites is chocolate pecan cheesecake." Lark punched Joey playfully on the arm.

Essie laughed. "Sounds like a recipe I'd like to have."

He stopped suddenly and ran his hand through his hair. "I don't mean to be bothering you all the time," he apologized. "I usually pick up Joey at Jamie's house, but I saw Miss Ida Belle at the grocery store, and she said they weren't home yet. I assumed this is where they would be." He motioned to Joey. "Come along, Bud, we have to go get that haircut."

"Ugh," Joey grunted, pulling away from his dad.

"Tough world, kiddo," he said with a chuckle. "Maybe we'll go out for pizza at Uncle Ziggy's later."

Joey brightened. "Can Jamie come, too?"

"We'll have to ask Miss Ida. Come on, Jamie, I'll drop you off and see what your grandma says." He paused a moment. "Maybe we should ask Miss Essie to join us?"

Both boys' eyes opened wide. "Yeah, yeah. Please come with us, Miss Essie," they said in harmony.

"Uncle Ziggy's got the bestest pizza in the whole wide world," Joey said.

Essie could feel Lark's eyes on her. Forcing herself to look away, she quieted the beating of her heart by holding her breathing to short intakes.

"How about it?" Lark asked. "We have a great pizza place. Would you like to go with us? You do like pizza, don't you?"

"Doesn't everyone love pizza, but . . ." Essie trailed off.

Lark looked at Joey and winked. "Good. I'll pick you up around seven."

Essie put on a pair of her favorite jeans and sweatshirt and was waiting when Lark showed up right at seven o'clock. The boys jumped into the small seat in the extended cab behind the driver. Essie climbed into the truck beside Lark and snapped her seat belt shut.

"Glad to see where the bank is and that you have a library," she said as she gazed out the window on the way to Uncle Ziggy's. "And I appreciate the invitation," she said. "I haven't learned my way around town yet."

"I'll be glad to show you around if you like," Lark offered. "It should only take about thirty minutes of my time."

"I'm beginning to like the small-town atmosphere, though. It's so quiet and peaceful. I think I've met more people since moving here than I had friends in Tulsa."

"I agree with you. A big city is not an environment that I want to raise Joey in."

"Have you ever lived in a city?" she asked.

"I was in Seattle for about two years. The only good thing to come of it was that's where I met my wife, Jane. We planned to go back to Carson, my hometown, but when Jane got sick, we stayed to be close to her doctors. After she was gone, I got out of there as fast as I could."

Lark glanced out the window, and Essie could detect the sadness in his voice. "Oh, Lark." She laid her hand on his arm. "I'm so sorry. Do you mind if I ask what was wrong with her?"

"About six months after we were married, we decided to take a trip to the Black Hills as one last excursion before we settled into our careers. Jane was already pregnant with Joey, and we wanted to be ready to welcome our baby and to become model parents." He adjusted his mirror, glancing at the preoccupied boys in the back seat, and spoke quietly. "When we got home, she wasn't feeling well, so she went to the doctor. She was diagnosed with cancer, already in advanced stages. Because she was pregnant, there wasn't anything more they could do for her without hurting the baby. She refused treatment, and six months after Joey was born, she lost her battle." His voice wavered as he spoke.

"How awful! How did you manage with a six-month-old baby?" Essie's voice cracked, and she felt the lump in her throat.

"I moved back to Carson with my parents. I was a wreck, but my mother was wonderful. I taught in a small rural school for a year. When this job was offered to me, I jumped at it. Mrs. Pearson, who lives over on the west side of town, practically raised Joey until he started school. I was lucky to find her." He sighed heavily. "I've never regretted moving here for one moment."

When Lark parked the car outside the pizza place, the boys jumped out and ran ahead of them. By the time Lark and Essie got inside, Joey and Jamie were already seated at a table and munching on a bowl of complimentary roasted peanuts. Lark and Essie crunched across the floor on the empty shells, and Lark pulled out a chair for her.

"One thing the boys like about this place is that they can throw things on the floor and not get yelled at." Lark smirked at the boys, and they grinned back at him.

The waitress brought a menu and they decided what they wanted and ordered.

"You guys better slow down on those peanuts, or you won't have any room left for pizza," Lark warned.

"I got plenty of room left," Joey said. "I'm so hungry I could eat a whole pizza." He rubbed his stomach.

Lark rolled his eyes upward. "You're always hungry. You're going to eat me into poverty."

Essie reached over and patted Joey on the head. "He's just a growing boy."

"I know, and I've got how many years ahead of me to feed him? You're getting a job when you're nine, kid," he teased.

The waitress brought the pizza, and everyone dug in. The boys, true to their word, ate their share. They were almost ready to go when Essie spotted a woman coming up behind Lark and putting her hands on his shoulders. She watched Lark jerk at the touch before he looked up at the woman standing behind him.

"Diana." He immediately turned and took her hand.

Essie paid close attention as she waited to be introduced. The woman had long blonde hair that was pulled back into a ponytail, enhancing the beauty of her perfect complexion. Somehow in those hazel eyes, Essie could see a shattering hint of sadness as the beautiful woman gazed at Lark with an expression of tenderness.

Lark drew Diana around beside him, still holding onto her hand. "Diana, I'd like for you to meet Essie. Essie is Miss Tessie's granddaughter. She's new in town, and we were just introducing her to the best pizza she's ever tasted."

"I can't argue with that," Essie said, nodding from across the table. "It's nice to meet you, Diana."

"Diana is a colleague of mine. She teaches those, shall we say, very active fifth graders."

"More like rambunctious," Diana said. She turned to Essie with what appeared to be a hint of hesitancy. "It's nice to meet you. Welcome to Rosepoint." She held up a pizza box, emitting the aroma of sausage, Italian spices, and mushrooms. "I'd better go before my pizza gets cold." Giving Lark's shoulder a slight squeeze, she turned to leave.

Lark pushed his chair back. "You boys, get ready to go. I'll walk with Diana to her car." He pointed his finger at the boys. "And leave a few peanuts for the next person."

The boys grinned and grabbed the dish of peanuts, putting them into their pockets. Jamie whispered into Joey's ear, then giggled, took one peanut out, and placed it in the dish.

Essie watched curiously as Lark and Diana walked out of the restaurant. The ease with which they connected caused a tiny tug in Essie's heart.

Lark returned shortly. The boys, pockets bulging with peanuts, erupted in giggles. "Get out of here, you little scoundrels," Lark said with a grin, pushing them fondly toward the door.

Essie followed them, unsure of the feelings that arose in her chest.

The next morning as Essie drank her second cup of coffee, she looked outdoors to see Pete unloading several pieces of lumber and a box of tools from his *Toyota 4Runner*. She poked her head out the door.

"Good morning," Pete called out as he threw the last piece of lumber on the ground.

"Good morning." Amazed at the large number of materials he'd brought with him, she said, "I thought you said it would only take a piece or two of lumber to fix these."

"I always come prepared. You never know what problem you'll run into."

"I *am* going to pay you for that lumber," she said with a stern voice. "Your labor, too, if you'll let me."

"It's just a few pieces I found lying around. Don't worry about it." He picked up the lumber and walked toward the broken steps.

"I see that! Is that why *Johnson's Hardware and Supply* is stamped on the side of the planks?" she asked.

Pete shrugged. "Must have been some Frank threw out. Maybe a little too crooked to sell."

Essie pressed her lips tight together and shook her head. "Can I at least get you a cup of coffee before you build my steps out of that crooked lumber?"

"I would love a cup. Just black is fine." He turned for a second trip to his truck.

She went inside and poured him a cup of coffee, put a couple of cookies on a saucer, and took them out to him. "Remind me before you go home that I have a plate of goodies to send with you, courtesy of the good ladies of this town."

"That alone is enough pay. I better get busy and earn them."

Pete worked the rest of the morning and part of the afternoon. Essie had a completely new set of steps leading up to her back porch. She made ham sandwiches for lunch, and they sat and ate together at an old picnic table in the backyard. Afterward, Pete straightened the shutters on the front of the house and fastened them so they wouldn't shift in the wind. Essie sent him off with his plate of sweets and his promise of returning tomorrow to paint the new steps before it rained.

The next morning, Pete showed up at the house early with a brush and a can of paint.

"And I suppose you found that just lying around." Essie bounced down the steps and gave Pete a big hug.

"Yeah, something like that," he said. Pete held the can out for her to see a splash of bright green paint streaked across the top. "I hope this color will be okay."

"What!" she hollered. "Mr. Pete, are you colorblind? You can't paint my steps green. It won't match anything." Her mouth was agape, and her eyes opened wide as she looked at him in disbelief.

Ignoring her, Pete opened the can, coated the brush, and spread a pale gray layer on the steps.

She ran to him and slapped him hard on his shoulder. "Why you . . . you almost gave me a heart attack."

He laughed, rubbing his shoulder. "Just keeping you on your toes."

By noon, Pete had two coats of paint on the steps. As they sat down at the old, weathered picnic table to eat the tuna-hotdish she'd made, she felt like they were two old friends having lunch together.

"So how did you enjoy *Uncle Ziggy's Pizza*?" He glanced over at her, awaiting her answer.

Essie looked up, a frown on her face. "How did you know I went for pizza?"

Pete chuckled. "You forget, this is a small town."

"Oh, so you were the one following us. We talked about calling the cops." She shook her finger at him. "You're lucky you're not sitting in the county jail, Mr. Pete."

"And I thought I was being so discreet. Guess I'll have to reassess my skills as a private eye." He scraped his plate, took the last bite, and pushed it toward Essie.

"Seriously though, how did you know?" She got up and started to clear the table.

"I ran into Diana this morning. She told me she met you." He stacked the plates and handed them to her.

"Yes, we did meet."

"She's a nice lady. Such a sad story, though," Pete said.

"Okay, you have my curiosity. So tell me about her." Her heart gave a small leap.

He balled his napkin into a wad and threw it at her with a silly grin on his face. "Like you weren't curious before. Like you didn't want to ask me if she and Lark were dating."

"I did not! But are they?" She giggled and threw the napkin back at him.

"Lark's been a good friend to Diana through all this mess. Her husband had an affair with a young woman over in Hampton, and they took off together. The bad part about it was that he didn't seem to care who knew. Diana was so embarrassed by the whole situation. Besides, I think she really loved the guy, in spite of what he did to her."

"So she latched on to Lark to save herself embarrassment?" Essie wondered aloud. "Does she and her husband have children?"

"No. If they had, it might have made a difference. Rumors are his girlfriend is pregnant."

"What about you? Do you have a girlfriend?" Essie asked with a smirk.

Pete laughed. "No, I'm like, God, I love them all. But I guess you could say I'm a confirmed bachelor."

Essie went over to him and gave him a warm hug. "Thank you for being my friend. I really miss my sidekick, Emma, back in Tulsa. I still talk to her, but it's not like being face to face."

"Well, I'm here for you, and woe to that person who tries to do you wrong." He squeezed her back and pushed her gently away.

"Thanks, I appreciate it. I'll need some advice when I start remodeling. I tend to let people run all over me."

"Not anymore. You can count on me. But honestly, I really don't know what kind of relationship is going on between Lark and Diana. I say if he's interested in you, you'll know. Lark's a good guy, and he'll be honest with you. He won't hurt either of you if he can help it."

Essie shook her head, her cheeks heating up. "Lark has no interest in me. He asked me along because he was being nice. It was obvious he and Diana have something going." She looked to Pete for his opinion.

"I'm not so sure about that," Pete said. "If someone needs him, he'll be there for them. He's that kind of guy. Diana needed help, and he was there for her."

"And I hear the same thing about you, Mr. Pete, the first one on the job handyman."

Pete grinned. "I'm first because I run faster." He grabbed the casserole and followed her into the kitchen.

"No, that's because you're a goodhearted man."

"Speaking of running, this goodhearted man better ske-daddle." He gave her a hug and left.

It was about time for the boys to show up, and Essie was delighted to surprise them. She strained as she lifted the old chair up the stairs from the basement, one step at a time, struggling to keep it anchored so she wouldn't go tumbling back down. The chair would be perfect for the boys' clubhouse. She eased it up the last step and expelled a big sigh of relief as she pushed it onto the kitchen floor. Sliding it out of the way into the corner, she could almost see the surprise on their faces.

"I found another item for your clubhouse," Essie said to them when they came walking over from Miss Ida's where Lark dropped them.

"What's a item?" Joey asked with a puzzled look on his face.

"An item means a thing. It's just another word we use. You stay right here, and I'll bring it to you." She went inside to get the chair.

"Oh boy," Joey said as they pushed the old chair into the shed. "We're getting everything fancy. Maybe we can sleep out here one night. It'll be just like camping."

"Now we'll both have our own chair," Jamie said, plopping down on their new addition. "Joey, did you know your dad is a item?"

Joey giggled. "My dad's not a item. He's my dad."

"I heard Mr. Bass and Miss Anderson talking at school one day, and they said your dad and Miss Diana was a item."

Essie cupped her hand over her mouth and quickly stepped back inside. She couldn't help but wonder at the minds of these young boys as she listened to their innocent chatter, giggling so hard she had to go wash her face.

27

"Tomorrow's my turn to take a treat to school. My item is picking me up here to go buy cookies," Joey said, doubling over in laughter. He fell to the floor dramatically and kicked his heels in the air.

Quickly diverting the subject and hoping they would forget, Essie hollered out to them. "Hey, boys, how would you like to make your cookies instead of buying them?"

They both jumped up and came running to her. "Can we, really?"

"We sure can. What kind would you like to make? We can either make chocolate chip or we could make snicker-doodles?"

"Let's do snickerdoodles. Everybody always brings chocolate chip," Jamie said.

"We better hurry then." Essie glanced at her watch. "What time is your dad picking you up?"

"He said he'd be a little late. He has a meeting after school," Joey said.

"Okay, we better get started then. You go wash your hands. I'll get everything ready here."

The boys took turns stirring and measuring. When they were ready, she showed them how to roll the dough into small balls, dip them in the cinnamon and sugar mix, then place them on the cookie sheet. They all sat down to wait for the cookies to bake.

The boys met Lark at the door, anxious to surprise him. He deeply inhaled as he entered the house. The sweet aroma of cinnamon hung in the air as Essie took the cookies out of the oven and put them on racks to cool.

"Daddy, we don't have to go buy cookies," Joey said. "Miss Essie and us made snickerdoodles." He grabbed his dad's hand and led him to the kitchen.

Essie had found three boxes and was busy arranging the cookies between wax paper.

"It smells delicious, but you didn't ask Miss Essie to do this, did you?" Lark asked with concern.

"Totally my idea, I assure you," Essie said. "I heard Joey say you were going to the store to get treats for school. I thought this would be a good secret club project." She winked at Lark. "Besides, we had lots of fun, huh, boys?"

"Yeah," they both echoed.

"Can we have a cookie?" Joey asked.

"Of course. What was I thinking? All this hard work and no reward. But only one before supper." She gave them each a cookie and sent them to the clubhouse.

Lark came close to her and laid his hand on her shoulder. "I really appreciate you doing this and spending time with the boys, but I'm concerned they're interfering with your time."

As his gaze caught hers and held it, she blushed at the thought of him hearing her heartbeat. She quickly turned her head. "I love spending time with them. They're both a delight. I guess it's because I never had a best friend when I was growing up. I have so much fun just watching them together."

"Not even a brother or sister?" Lark asked.

"No. I had a brother, but he died when I was about three. I don't remember him at all."

He looked at her, shaking his head. "Don't tell me you didn't have friends. I can't believe that."

She laughed. "Oh, I had friends, just not a best friend. I've been meaning to ask you, what about Jamie? Does he have siblings? And what about his parents? Why is he living with his grandmother?"

"As long as I've been here, Jamie's lived with his grandmother. I believe she adopted him when he was just a baby. Miss Ida never talks about her son. I don't think the mother is in the picture in any way."

"Miss Essie, can we have another cookie?" Jamie shyly

asked as he came into the kitchen with Joey in tow.

"Remember, I told you only one. But I do have a little box for each of you to take home. But only after supper, okay?"

Jamie nodded his head as she handed each of them a box and a bigger box to Lark.

Pointing her finger at him, she said, "And you, remember, these are for Joey's treat."

"Yes, ma'am, Miss Essie, I'll remember." Lark stood straight and saluted her military style. "But I think I better drop Jamie off, or I'm not sure how many of his will make it home with him." He ruffled Jamie's wild hair. "You and Joey go get in the truck, and I'll give you a ride."

"I see you have new steps," Lark commented as he went out the door. "Let me guess, Pete?"

"Yes, he's unstoppable. I told him I would get someone to do all this stuff. He doesn't listen very well."

Lark shook his head and chuckled. "I told you he was hard to get rid of."

Lark could almost hear his heart beating as he dropped Jamie off, and he and Joey made their way home. This unfamiliar feeling for another woman brought guilt to his mind. It had been almost seven years since he'd lost his wife, Jane, and in that time, he'd devoted his every hour to raising Joey. He and Jane were so in love, and when she passed so suddenly, he vowed to keep his promise to her to love and cherish their tiny son, the only part of her left with him. He thought of Diana at Uncle Ziggy's and shivered when he thought of how it must have looked to Essie. When her husband left town with another woman, Diana, a beautiful and classy lady, became utterly devastated, and Lark, feeling sorry for her, went to her and offered to be a companion to her to keep the wolves away. Diana was overwhelmingly embarrassed by the situation, so

Lark promised to keep their true relationship a secret. As an added benefit, it would squelch any rumors of his availability. Until now, the arrangement had worked just fine.

Chapter Three

As Essie wandered around the spacious rooms so full of memories, she pondered over the tasks that loomed before her. She had all of Nana's personal belongings to dispose of or to find a suitable place for. Plundering through the closets, she recognized a fuzzy blue robe that she'd bought her nana several years ago. She remembered her nana unwrapping it at Christmas, then putting it on and parading around in front of everyone. Essie didn't know if her nana really loved the robe or if she played it up for Essie's sake. Nevertheless, as a teenager, it made an impression on Essie. Every Christmas thereafter, Nana never failed to show up sometime during their visit in that robe. As an adult now, Essie understood the little sacrifices and thoughtful gestures that had been extended for her benefit.

She buried her face in the robe's softness, relishing the aroma of her nana and the sweet memories it brought back to her. With tears in her eyes, she slipped the robe over her pajamas. This was one article of clothing she'd definitely found a suitable place for.

On the top shelf above the clothing, she noticed what looked like an album. Standing on her tiptoes, she reached for it, pulled it from the shelf, and sat down to look at it. The album was filled with pictures of her as a baby with her mom and dad and with Nana and Grandpa. All her grade school pictures were arranged in order of age, and pictures of her with Nana every Christmas were laid neatly displayed on the old pages.

Further into the album, she found pictures of herself graduating from high school, and later, snapshots from college with short notations written underneath in her nana's distinguished handwriting. Funny how different she looked now. As a younger woman, her dark brown hair hung almost to her waist. Her light blue eyes were much darker now. She recalled the first time she got her hair cut, how she'd cried for hours until her friend, Emma, labeled the new style *The Perky Flip* with sassy curls around her ears.

"It fits you perfectly, girlfriend," Emma had assured her.

Enough of this, she thought as she returned the album to its proper place. If she reacted to everything in this manner, she'd be a sniffling mess by the time she got through all her nana's things. The corner of another album sticking out drew her attention. She pulled the album down and found it to be an almost identical version of the other one, except this album featured younger versions of Mom and Dad, and of Nana and Grandpa. As she turned the pages, it became clear that this was an album her nana had put together of her brother, Tory. He'd been a handsome young fellow and wore a big smile on his face in every photo. The pictures of Tory stopped abruptly at what looked like about the age of sixteen years old.

As she studied the pictures, she tried to imagine what it would be like to have a brother, or anyone at all for that matter. She'd lost her mom and dad almost five years ago in a car accident. She wished she could have known her brother. She thought of Joey and Jamie and how much she adored being around them. How sad for her mom and dad and for her grandparents. How sad for anyone to lose a child. She swallowed the lump she felt forming in her throat and pushed herself to continue the many duties she had facing her.

As Essie walked through the big house, she became more and more aware of what the responsibilities of a homeowner really entailed. Every room she entered looked dark and dreary and in dire need of new paint. She could see in one of the upstairs bedrooms where water leaking through the roof left brown stains on the ceiling. Down in the kitchen, almost all the doors on the cabinets hung loose, and the drawers squeaked when she opened them. She knew she needed to find a contractor, but she had no idea how to go about it. Pete would be the one to help her, but she didn't want to impose on him, as she knew he would insist on doing a lot of it himself. Maybe she could ask Lark if he knew anyone, or would Pete get mad? He'd made it quite clear he was there to help.

She jotted down a list of repairs that needed to be done. The outside of the large home posed a big project. The house hadn't been painted in years. She took a deep breath and slowly exhaled as she thought of restoring the house to the fairy tale castle it had once been in her childhood. Bringing herself back to reality, it was almost time for the boys, and she chuckled at how much she looked forward to seeing them almost every evening.

As they came running through the yard at high speed, Essie listened to them chattering excitedly. Their class had been chosen to participate in an all-school play night. Practicing for weeks, they'd performed in front of their class, but now they'd earned the opportunity to show their talents to their friends and family.

"Will you come see us? Please, Miss Essie. Me and Joey are both in it. Just wait till you see us. I'm the star!" Jamie giggled and puffed out his chest.

"Of course, I'll go. I wouldn't miss it. What's the name of your play?"

"Pushkin Goes to School. Jamie's a dog." Joey patted Jamie on the back and said, "Nice doggie."

"And I'll bet you're a good dog. What part do you play, Joey?" Essie asked.

"I'm the teacher," Joey said proudly.

"That's cause his dad's a teacher, and he knows how,"

Jamie explained.

"Of course, he's a good teacher. I can't wait to see it. What night is it?"

"It's tomorrow night. My dad said he'd pick you up if you wanted to go," Joey said.

Her heart skipped a beat at the thought of going anywhere with Lark. "Tell him I'll drive. I'm sure he needs to be there early to help get you ready."

"My dad don't have to do nothing. Mrs. Jordan is our play teacher."

"Yeah, but he kinda helps her," Jamie added

"Does Mrs. Jordan teach at school, or does she just come in to help with the play?" Essie asked.

Jamie looked puzzled. "You know, you met her when we got pizza."

It took Essie a minute to understand what they meant.

Mrs. Jordan. Diana. *I'll bet he does kind of help her*, she thought.

On the evening of the play, Essie got a call from Pete.

"Jamie told me you were going to drive to school. No need for that. I'm going right by your house, so I'll pick you up,"

"Thank you, I was a little nervous about going alone," Essie admitted.

"I thought you were probably going with Lark," he commented.

She groaned. "He did offer, smarty. But I figured he'd be all tied up with Diana and the play. It seems she's their *play teacher* as the boys put it."

"You sound a little jealous."

"I'm not jealous," she said loudly. "I told you Lark's not interested in me."

"Yeah, yeah! I'll pick you up at six-thirty."

Essie smiled as she laid the phone on the table. Pete to the rescue again. She was amazed at how relaxed she felt around him. If he had any intentions toward her other than being a friend, he certainly hadn't shown them. She made up her mind. Tonight, she would use some of that help he so generously offered. She would ask him for advice about her restoration project.

Essie took a leisurely bath in the old claw foot bathtub where many of her dreams as a child had taken root. She remembered her nana wrapping her in a warm fluffy towel and sprinkling her with powder. She could almost feel her nana's arms around her and smell the sweet aroma of lavender as she snuggled close to her warm body. The nostalgia felt almost overwhelming as her mind flooded with childhood memories.

Considering the chill in the air, she dressed in a lightweight lavender sweater and a pair of plum-colored pants. She waited anxiously in the foyer until Pete showed up for her at six-thirty. The anxiety didn't lessen as they made their way to the school.

Surprised to see so many people streaming into the small school, Essie glanced around in awe. "It looks like the whole town is here. I thought it would be mostly parents."

Pete took her arm and guided her toward the front door of the school. "I told you it was a friendly place. Besides, almost everyone is either related or a neighbor. This is the way we all support each other."

They took their seats in the small auditorium and waited. The hustle and bustle brought back memories of her own school days. Anxious little eyes peeked from behind the stage curtain, checking to see if their loved ones were there, and when they spotted them, a wave of enthusiasm to their proud parents.

When the lights dimmed, the crowd quieted down in anticipation of seeing their little stars being born. The principal welcomed everyone and then announced, "Now, give a big hand of thanks to the lady who's responsible for all this . . . Diana Jordan."

Pete looked over at Essie, and she quickly looked away.

Diana came onto the stage and took the microphone. Dressed in a pale green pantsuit, with her long blonde hair pulled back into a ponytail that hung down one side of her shoulder, she looked classy and beautiful.

Why wouldn't Lark be interested in her? Essie thought.

Essie sat too far away to see Lark's reaction to Diana's speech. She pictured herself sitting there beside Lark, encouraging Jamie and Joey in their roles, and being introduced proudly to all his colleagues as his girlfriend. She knew Diana as a constant companion to Lark, but had he ever referred to her as his girlfriend?

The play, short and sweet, told the story of Pushkin, a lonely little pug puppy who followed her buddy to school one day. The children in the school talked their teacher into letting Pushkin stay in their class. The students tried to teach Pushkin to add by barking her answer. Laughter rang out constantly from the audience as the children put forth their best efforts. Jamie played his part of the puppy Pushkin perfectly, and Joey, as the compassionate yet stern teacher, excelled. At the end of the play, the audience stood and broke into applause.

Soon the boys and the rest of the children ran out from behind the stage. Hugs and compliments on their performances were extended to them by all. Out of the corner of her eye, Essie could see Lark heading her way. She took a quick breath, cheeks already pinking, when Lark abruptly stopped and turned sharply back toward the stage.

From the far corner of the auditorium came the sound of angry voices, a male and female, rising above the noise of the thinning crowd. From where Essie stood, she could see Diana near the stage, clearly upset and gesturing gruffly to a man beside her. She watched as Lark hurried up to the two, seeming to confront the man face to face. Words were spoken, and the man turned in a huff and headed toward the door.

Essie's heart sank as she watched Lark put his arm around Diana. Diana, clearly distraught, laid her head heavily on his shoulder. Lark glanced back, his eyes catching Essie's, but then too quickly, he returned his attention back to Diana. It seemed like the rest of the townsfolk were far too busy chit-chatting and visiting to notice what had just transpired.

Essie felt certain she'd seen something she shouldn't. She shook her head to clear the distracting thoughts and turned to the excited little boys bouncing around her. She spotted Miss Ida whispering to Joey and watched a broad grin spread across his face.

He ran up to Jamie, grabbed him by the hands, and exclaimed, "Jamie, your grandma said I could stay over at your house tonight 'cause we wouldn't sleep anyway 'cause we're too 'cited, and it's not a school night anyway. But I have to go ask Daddy. Come on, go with me." The two boys ran across the floor, ducking and swerving through the chattering crowd. Essie watched as Lark turned their way, Diana still on his arm. Miss Ida gave him a confirming wave, and the boys came racing back across the floor.

As they left, Pete put his arm around Essie's shoulder and guided her through the door. Because she'd turned down a ride from Lark, had Pete somehow misinterpreted this as a date, or even worse yet, had Lark thought she was out with Pete?

Essie fought hard to erase the scene of Lark and Diana from her mind as they drove home. How long had they been together? What right did she have to waltz into town and expect him to sever his previous relationships? It was about time Essie began concentrating on the things she needed to do.

"I'm ready to find a contractor and start the renovations. I need advice bad. Would you be my adviser?" she asked.

"My pleasure," Pete said. "Why don't I come over, and we can go through what you want done. Then you can decide where to go from there?"

Pulling a big breath of air into her lungs, she exhaled a sigh of relief. She savored the idea of having Pete on her team. Organization was a trait she fell short on. "Sounds good, but please do this at your own leisure. I don't want to take you away from anything you have planned."

"Oh, then since you're not in a hurry, how about I stop by in a couple of months?" The twinkle in his eye lightened Essie's mood.

She elbowed him gently in the ribs. "On second thought, you're fired. I'll see if I can find someone reliable."

The next morning, Pete came knocking at Essie's door before she'd even finished breakfast. He greeted her with a salute. "Your most dependable planner and organizer reporting for duty, ma'am."

"Good morning! You're up bright and early, I see." She snugged her nana's robe around her.

"I hear someone here has some renovating to do. I'm anxious to get started." Pete stood looking at her with a silly grin on his face.

"Obviously more so than I am." Essie pointed to her bowl of oatmeal. "Have you eaten?"

"Two hours ago. I can't sleep when there's important work to be done."

She slapped him on the back as she went to put her bowl in the sink.

"Okay, shall we start upstairs, and you can do your important work while I change from my pajamas?" They climbed the stairs, and she pointed to a couple of doors. "You can look around in there for a start. I know for sure the roof has a leak in one room. I'll be out shortly."

Essie finished changing and hurried back to the room where she'd left Pete. She stood just in the doorway and watched him. It was a spacious room that was furnished with a full-sized bed, a dresser, and two faded blue chairs. The bed, covered with a quilt detailed with squares of animals, airplanes, trucks, and tractors, was obviously made special for someone. At the foot of the bed sat a small wooden chest. She quietly watched as Pete rubbed his fingers over the chest as he knelt beside it, lifting the lid. Reaching inside, he took out a worn baseball bat and fingered it, quickly putting it back as he looked up and saw her standing there.

"It looks like this one only needs paint or wallpaper and new carpeting. Are you planning on modernizing it or trying to restore it to its original condition?" Pete asked, clearing his throat.

"I want to keep it as original as possible. As you can probably tell, this was my brother Tory's room."

"You never mentioned to me that you have a brother." Pete's brow raised as he stood.

"I don't. I was only three when he died. After that, my nana wouldn't change a thing in here. Wouldn't let anyone sleep in here either. I think I'd like to repaper all the bedrooms, and especially the parlor, but I don't know what I'll do with this room. Maybe I'll just keep it like Nana wanted."

Pete looked around at the slanted ceiling and down at the short walls. "Have you ever tried to find hidden spaces in these walls? Many of the older homes have secret storage that way."

She laughed. "I hardly think my nana would have hidden rooms or secret passageways. You make it sound like a gory old castle or something."

He began to tap on the wall, listening intently and bending

down to examine the panels.

The melodic chiming of the doorbell brought Essie back to the moment, interrupting their joshing. "I wonder who that could be? You keep on searching for the hidden treasure while I go answer the door." She giggled. "Maybe that's where Nana hid all of her gold bars."

Essie ran down the stairs and could see Lark through the glass pane of the door, pacing the porch. Feeling the usual pitter-patter of her heart, she took a deep breath and opened the door. "Good morning."

"Good morning. I hope I'm not bothering you so early in the morning."

"No, you're too late for that. Pete already beat you to it." She chuckled. "Please come in." She stepped back and motioned for him to enter.

"I'm sorry. If you're busy, I can come back. I'm sure Pete wouldn't want me hanging around."

She shook her head, gesturing toward the sofa. "Pete's over helping me decide on a contractor and what needs to be done with the house. I'm really excited to get started."

"I just came by to say I'm sorry I didn't get to say hello last night. There was a matter I had to take care of."

"I saw that. I hope everything's okay with Diana." Watching his reactions closely, she waited for an explanation.

Hesitating briefly, he stared intently at Essie. "I think the matter is taken care of. She'll be fine." He sat back, stretching his long arm across the back of the sofa. "I hope you enjoyed the boys' play. They were happy you came."

"I did. I wouldn't have missed it for anything. Looks like you might have a little actor on your hands."

Lark laughed softly, tipping his head to one side. "He's a little actor, all right. I'm not sure it's something that would carry him very far in life, though."

"I have a feeling Joey will be able to do anything he wants

to. He's a smart little boy."

"I'll let you get back to your business." Lark stood to go and took her hand in his. "If I can be of help in any way, let me know." His eyes held hers.

"Thanks. I don't want to bother anyone."

He wrinkled his brow and looked sideways at her with a smirk on his face. "You don't seem to mind bothering Pete." He hesitated a moment. "But I'm sure Pete has everything under control," he said quickly. "He knows much more about that sort of thing than I do."

Essie nodded. "I promise if I need anything, I'll let you know."

Lark suddenly turned as he walked toward the door. "Oh, I just wanted to mention that if Joey and Jamie ever say anything about going to the old Sawyer place, just down the road from here, don't let them. It's an old, abandoned house, which is sometimes intriguing to kids. I don't want to start any rumors, but there's something a little strange going on there. Probably just some kids fooling around, but you never know."

Essie felt chills running through her body. She'd seen places like that, and the thought of Jamie and Joey going near it made her shiver. "I'll keep an eye on them. I'm sure it isn't as bad here, but in Tulsa, a place like that would be a haven for drug dealing."

"I certainly hope not, but I know it's a possibility." He put his hand on her shoulder and softly slid it down to her elbow. "I'll let you get back to Pete. I'm sure he's wondering where you are." Outside, he waved and slowly walked away.

What am I doing here? Lark thought to himself as he walked back to his truck. *Every time I see her, she's with Pete. I offered to pick her up for the boys' play, yet she chose to go with Pete. I've known Pete ever since he's been in town, and of all the women who threw themselves at him, I've never known him to date any one of them.*

He recalled watching Pete with his arm around Essie just as he started toward her, but then the thing with Diana had happened. Loud noises rose above the crowd as he turned and saw Diana talking with a man in the far corner near the stage. He'd gone to her rescue, making it quite clear to the man that he needed to leave. It had been an old acquaintance of her husband's, slightly inebriated, insisting that she go out with him.

This was a different feeling altogether for Lark, and he didn't know if he knew how to play the role. Being the only child, he'd gone off to college and graduated high in his class. There was never any doubt in his mind about what he wanted to do. He'd worked with younger kids his last two years in high school. He met Jane on a trip to Seattle, and after graduation, he secured a teaching job and moved there. After they were married, plans were to move back to Carson. Jane was an orphan, so she was excited to relocate to a smaller town and to be near her new in-laws.

Jane's pregnancy surprised them both, but they embraced it with enthusiasm. When the doctor diagnosed her with cancer, their world fell apart. After consultation with the doctor, they were informed the baby could not survive the harsh chemo Jane would need to merely keep her alive. Not once did Jane consider the idea of undergoing anything that would harm the baby. In her own words, *"It is my way of leaving behind a part of me to always be a part of you."*

It was the hardest thing Lark had ever encountered. The first year, the only thing to come close to putting a smile on his face was Joey. He insisted on devoting his every moment to caring for him, although his mother tried to help all he would allow.

Not once in all these almost eight years did Lark think about dating another woman, nor did he consider himself burdened. And certainly not lonely. His lips parted in a huge smile as he thought about the chatty little boy that looked so much like his mom.

And as for Diana — when her husband Jim hurt her so badly, he could see the effects it was having on her. Normally a very social lady, she secluded herself from even the least of activity, and that was when Lark approached her with his idea of being an escort to her.

Not until he met Essie had things changed for him. His heart skipped a beat as he thought of his very first meeting with her and how it sent him reeling, but then there was Pete. Right away, he knew beyond doubt that he would fight in his own patient and gentile way to get to know her. And he also knew in the back of his mind that the promise he'd made to Diana would be a problem.

What a strange visit, she thought, as she headed back up the stairs to Pete. Had she not been busy, would he have stayed longer? Was it her imagination, or was he a little resentful of Pete?

Essie suddenly stopped as she entered the bedroom where she'd left Pete. The muscles in her body tightened as she saw Pete sitting there. Seated on the floor beside a panel he'd taken out of the wall, he held a small toy in his hand. He flicked away a tear from the corner of his eye.

She sat beside him on the floor and patted him on the back. "I can't believe you found this. How did you know? What did you find in there?"

He held out the little toy truck he had in his hand. "This must have been your brother's hideaway."

Taking the little red truck from him, she rubbed her hand softly over it, grieving for the brother she would never know.

"Here, let me show you something." He crawled over to

the opening in the wall and pointed to a sign that read Prince Tory's Castle, painted on cardboard in a childlike scribble, and tacked to the opening.

A lump formed in Essie's throat. "I wonder if Nana knew this was here." She knelt beside the opening and peeked in. Running several feet in both directions, dark and eerie inside, she could see an old blanket and a small pillow. It was her brother's make-believe bed. She smiled widely to know her brother had been born with the same sense of imagination as her.

"I think she knew this was here. That's why she wanted to keep this room the way it was and not change anything," Pete said. "That's so sad. Tell me about your brother." Sitting flat on the floor, he drew his knees up and crossed his arms over them. His eyes met hers.

"I hardly remember him. He was quite a bit older than me. He must have been a teenager." Essie said. "His name was Tory. One day Mom just told me he was gone, and they never talked about him. But thank you for caring."

"I know what it's like, losing family," he said quietly.

At that time, Essie felt a strange aura around Pete, and she couldn't make herself delve further into his past.

After sitting motionless for a moment, Pete jumped to his feet. "Well, we'll keep this as a memorial to him." He put the little truck back inside the wall and closed the panel.

They made a list of all the repairs to be done. Other than the painting, wallpapering, and carpeting, most of the repairs were minor. "I know just the right person for this job. He's done painting for almost half the people in this town. He sub-contracts his papering. He'll treat you right," Pete said.

"And what about the little jobs? Will he do those, too?"

Pete's mouth broke into a wide grin. "I'm available. I can get references if you like."

Essie sighed heavily. "Mr. Pete! How did I know you

would say that?"

"Look, I'm very capable of doing these things, and it's hard to find someone responsible. All the contractors are interested in are the big jobs. So . . . am I hired?"

"Only if you let me pay you the same wage as the painters. I mean it, Pete. You've done enough for me," she said in her most convincing voice.

"How else can I be around such charming company?"

"You're impossible." She made an ugly face and stuck out her tongue. "I was going to ask if you heard anything about the Sawyer place and what's going on there?"

"No, why do you ask?"

"Lark told me to not let Joey and Jamie go anywhere near it. He said there were some strange things going on."

"Like what?" he asked, rubbing a hand at the back of his neck.

"He didn't say. That's why I asked. I thought maybe you'd heard."

"I don't pay too much attention to rumors. Probably just high school kids fooling around. What better place for a beer party?"

"You sound like you know all about beer parties. You never told me about your teenage years. I bet you were a tiger."

"No, not really." He glanced at his watch. "I have to go now and see if I can make a date with the painter to come over and talk to us."

"Pete, I'm sorry. I don't mean to pry."

He tweaked her nose playfully. "Then don't. I don't talk about it."

CHAPTER FOUR

W hile eating her supper that evening, Lark stopped by. As Essie opened the door, her lips widened into a broad grin as the familiar patter of her heart warmed her whole body. "Well, if it isn't the handsome schoolteacher."

He grinned, stepping back a little as she opened the door wider. "Flattery will get you nowhere. May I come in? I have something to discuss with you."

"Of course, please do." She noticed him glancing toward the table and her plate.

"I'm sorry. I'm disturbing your dinner. Please go ahead and eat."

"No, I'm just finishing. So, what's up?" She walked toward the parlor, and he followed her.

"Just a matter that came up at our coffee clutch this morning." He casually moved a magazine and sat on the arm of the big, overstuffed chair. "The rumor is that Matt Simmons is changing our community hall into a nightclub. That hall is the center of any activity that happens in this town. We use it for weddings, council meetings, picnics, or anything else where a big crowd gathers. It'll be a great loss if that happens. We have no place else to go."

She frowned, giving her shoulders a slight shrug. "Matt Simmons, who is he? And how can one man have that power? I don't understand."

"He owns the building. Anyone who uses it pays him a fee." Standing, Lark put his hand in his pocket and nervously jingled the coins.

Essie spread her hands, palms up. "Surely, he can't just take the town hall away. What about the town officials? Don't they have anything to say?"

"Unfortunately, they don't. It's outside the limits and privately owned."

"So, what can you do about it? There must be something." She sat on the edge of the sofa. He took a seat in the old wooden rocker across from her.

"We've called a meeting Monday evening at my house to see if we can come up with a plan. Of course, the first thing we'll do is go see Matt, to see how true these rumors are. We want as many people there as we can get. Please try to come. You're a part of this community now." He looked at her pleadingly.

"Of course I'll come," she assured him. "Is there anything I can do? Like bring cookies?"

"That would be great. Some of the other ladies are bringing snacks, too. I'll furnish the drinks. I make a mean pot of coffee."

"Always the gracious host, huh." She laughed.

"Did you know that your grandfather built the hall and sold it to Matt shortly before he died?" Lark asked.

"No, I didn't know that. Too bad he didn't keep it. We wouldn't have a problem."

"From what the old-timers say, he just wanted a place the people of Rosepoint could meet and socialize. Did you also know he donated the lumber for the church next door? The whole community got together and built it. Your grandfather was a generous man."

Shivers ran up her back. "And now this man wants to open a nightclub next to the church. I'm sure that wasn't my grandfather's intention." Her memories of him were few, but she would vow to do all she could to preserve his good name.

"And it's only a short distance from the school, too. I don't know what Matt's thinking. He has two children in that school. Hopefully, we can talk some sense into him."

"How well do you know Mr. Simmons? What kind of a man is he?"

"Not too well, and I don't like to judge people, but I've heard he's rather fond of the dollar." Lark pressed his lips together and shook his head.

"That sounds like one strike against us already." She'd intentionally used the word *us*. It felt so right.

He rose to his feet. "Maybe, but we'll see what we can do. I have to go now. I have a few more stops to make." He reached out and touched her lightly on the arm. "I'm really glad you're here. You add a sparkle to all our lives." His eyes held hers for a moment, then he gave her arm a slight squeeze and turned to go.

Essie treasured all those little touches and could feel herself becoming more and more intrigued with this charming schoolteacher.

She rose in the morning full of energy, humming along with her radio as she cooked oatmeal for breakfast. For the first time in a long while, she felt like she belonged. She would do all she could to help keep the community hall, and at the same time, honor her grandfather's wish.

As she got ingredients together for her cookies, she found herself wondering what she would wear to the meeting, and even thinking about getting her hair cut. She chuckled to herself when she realized what she was doing. Although vehemently denying it, her subconscious knew it was because Lark would be there.

The doorbell rang, and she almost dropped a carton of eggs on the floor.

"Oh geez!" Essie put the eggs down, dusted the flour from her hands, and went to answer the door.

Pete, holding a blue carnation, stood waiting. He held the flower out to her. "A flower for a grand dame," he said as he bowed in a formal way.

"Why, Sir Peter, how gracious of you to come calling and to consider me worthy of your leftover boutonniere." Shaking with laughter, she wrapped her arm around his shoulder and pushed him inside.

"It's still in good shape. Don't ever say Old Pete threw something away that could be recycled."

She took a small bowl, dribbled a little water in it, and dropped the flower in. "I take it you had a good time at your friend's wedding yesterday."

"I did, indeed. And I saw Jim, the painter I told you about. He wants to set up a date to come and talk to you."

She rubbed her hands together. "Oh boy, I can't wait to get started. How busy is he? I know it's a big job, but I'm like a kid before Christmas."

He laughed. "I can see that. He has a couple of small jobs he's obligated to finish, then he can start. With no interruptions, he should be able to do the complete job in two to three weeks." He walked over to the candy dish sitting on the dining table and helped himself to a mint.

"Wow! I'll have my fairy tale castle back. I only wish Nana could see it." She closed her eyes and envisioned her nana holding her hands, dancing in a tiny circle, stopping at each improvement, grinning her appreciation to Essie.

"I'm sure she knows. She'd be mighty proud of her granddaughter, I'm sure. It'll be a castle only fit for a fairy tale princess." Pete grinned. "I suppose we'll have to build a moat around it just to keep the suitors away."

She stretched out her hands, and her mouth broke into a wide grin. "No moat, just send them all my way."

"Lark said you were going to the meeting at his house Monday evening. I'll pick you up at six-thirty."

"You don't have to cart me around. I do have a car, you know."

"Do you know how to get to his house?" he asked with a smirk on his face.

She shrugged her shoulders. "Never thought about that." She made a face at Pete, thinking she could never get the better of him.

"Okay, I'll be over in a couple of days to get started on some of the other little jobs. And, like I said, I'll pick you up at six-thirty for that meeting."

"If I'm ever not here when you come, I'll leave the door unlocked. I need to get a haircut, and I want to stop in at the library."

He looked at her sternly. "If you're not home, I'll come back. Don't ever leave your door unlocked. Remember the Sawyer place," he scolded.

"I thought you weren't worried about the Sawyer place?" She turned and stared him squarely in the eyes.

"I'm not. I'm worried about your place. I'll see you at six-thirty tomorrow." He turned and strode leisurely off down the sidewalk.

Essie spent most of Monday afternoon preparing herself for the evening. She took a long, relaxing bath, fiddled with her hair until she got it just right, did her nails, and rumbled through her closet until she decided on a blouse with soft pink flowers and winter-white pants, suitable for a casual meeting, yet flattering enough to be a little sassy.

She inwardly scolded herself, Shame on you, Essie Euller.

As soon as she heard Pete's vehicle pull up outside, Essie hurried down the stairs, picked up her purse and jacket, and rushed to meet him on the porch. This would be her initiation into being a part of the town where her grandparents had left their mark, and she was determined to do what she could to preserve that legacy.

When they pulled up in front of Lark's house and parked, Essie wasn't surprised at what she saw. Lark's home looked almost exactly as she would have expected. It was a modest white cottage adorned with light blue shutters and sur- rounded by a neatly manicured lawn. It stood amid a row of similar structures stretching down the tree-lined street.

Lark met them at the door and invited them in. She stepped into the living room, appropriately scattered with folding chairs placed among the furniture to accommodate the ex- pected crowd. The furniture was clean and simple, definitely a man's pad, with no sign of unnecessary frivolity created by a woman's touch. Her neighbor, Mrs. Dawson, greeted her enthusiastically and introduced her to the other early arrivals.

"Where do you want these cookies? Just show me your kitchen, and I'll help with whatever you need," she said to Lark.

"Thanks, but we have everything under control." He led her through the dining room into the kitchen where Diana was busily arranging the goodies on a big platter.

She looks very familiar with the surroundings, Essie thought.

"Essie, you remember Diana," he asked, taking the plate and giving it to her.

"Yes, of course. Nice to see you again." Essie nodded to her, trying to hide the little inkling of jealousy that popped up inside her head.

"And you, too. Thank you for the cookies. I'm sure they'll be appreciated."

"I'd like to tell you how much I enjoyed the play," Essie said. "The kids did a wonderful job, and I'm sure a good part of that was due to your guidance."

"Weren't they wonderful? I love helping them develop their talents." Diana continued arranging the cookies.

"May I help you do something? Pour that mean cup of coffee Lark brags about." Essie grinned at Lark.

He blushed and quickly looked away.

"Thank you, but Lark and I have everything under control," Diana said with finality.

Maybe they had everything under control, but Essie wasn't so sure about herself. She excused herself and went to sit by Mrs. Dawson. Just how familiar was Diana with Lark's house? How many meals had she cooked in his kitchen? Diana certainly seemed to feel right at home.

The meeting went well, with several ideas discussed and three people appointed to go see Matt Simmons. They were to report back to the group with the results, and if there was no suitable solution, there would be another meeting scheduled.

When Pete dropped Essie off at home, she felt much more aware of the difference between the intricate governing of a big city and a small town like Rosepoint.

True to his promise, Pete arrived the next morning at ten minutes after nine, loaded with tools and all kinds of accessories to begin his part of the renovations.

"Late on your first day of a new job. Makes me wonder if I should have asked for more references," she teased. "You know I'll have to dock your wages."

"Just taking my break early. You owe me five minutes yet. So what do you think of how we do things here in Rosepoint?" he asked seriously.

"What do you mean?" She poured a cup of coffee and set it in front of Pete.

"The meeting last night." He sighed and turned to face her. "Look, Essie, why don't you just tell Lark how you feel about him?"

She turned away from him. "What do you mean?"

"You've already said that. What I mean is, anyone can see the way you look at him. Just tell him you like him," he urged.

She shrugged her shoulders and walked to the window. "It's that obvious, huh? I can't do that."

"Why not?" He spread his hands in question and waited for her answer.

She turned to face him. "What about Diana?"

"What about her? I could put in a good word for you. Let him make the choice of who he wants to date."

She reached out and grabbed his arm. "Don't you dare!" The fear in her voice was obvious. How much could she trust Pete, she wondered. She had always been one to stay away from controversy, and if Lark was dating Diana, she certainly didn't want to cause trouble.

"Let me know if you change your mind. My five minutes are up. I need to get to work before my boss docks me." He grinned, grabbed his tools, and headed for the stairs.

"I'll be gone for about an hour," she called after him. Essie had phoned for an appointment earlier to get her hair cut.

When she got to the beauty shop, Dee greeted her like an old friend. "Honey, you don't have to call. Just drop in, and if I'm not here, I'm probably out back with Cutter, my old hound dog." She grabbed her by the hand and led her over to the only other lady there.

"Claire, I want you to meet Essie Euller. She's Miss Tessie's granddaughter. This is my sister-in-law, Claire Rollins."

"Nice to meet you," Claire said.

"Essie's moved into her grandmother's house. You know, the big manse over on Oak Street," Dee explained.

"I know, the one down the road from the spooky Sawyer place. Speaking of that, have you heard what's been going on there? I met Teresa the other day, and she said her husband was coming home late one night, and he swore he saw weird flashing lights there at two in the morning."

"If you ask me, it's just a bunch of punk kids messing around," Dee said. "Anyway, I would keep my doors locked if I were you, Essie. You just never know."

Claire shook her head. "I wouldn't be surprised if the big boys from Chicago are moving in. Rosepoint is exactly the kind of place they like to set up operations. And before you know it, it's too late."

Essie felt a weird sensation inside her. "Funny, I thought I moved away from that when I left Tulsa. I feel so safe here in Rosepoint."

"Honey, you're not safe anywhere anymore, but it's a lot better behind locked doors." Dee patted her on the shoulders. "I hope we haven't gone and frightened you."

When Essie got back to the house, she could hear Pete pounding away in the upstairs bathroom. She went to join him.

"Back so soon?" He turned to face her. "Wow, fancying up for anyone in particular?" he teased.

"No, I can't help it if my hair grows. When it gets too long, I get it cut," she answered curtly.

"So what bit of gossip did you pick up from all the Rosepoint girls today?" Pete asked.

"The only Rosepoint girl I met today was Dee's sister-in-law."

"Claire? Then I can bet you didn't come away empty-handed. No need to subscribe to the local paper when she's around."

"The only thing she talked about was the Sawyer place. She has her own ideas of what's happening there."

"Oh, I'll bet she does, so tell me the latest. Seen any monsters prowling around?" He set his wrench down and waited for her to continue.

"What do you think is going on? Do the cops ever check it

out?" His teasing couldn't sidetrack her.

He laughed. "You mean Stan? About the only thing he checks out are the pretty girls."

"She said somebody saw some kind of weird lights flashing at two in the morning."

"Probably their eyes playing tricks on them. People should be asleep at that time of night."

She slapped him on the arm. "Don't you ever take anything seriously? I live three blocks from a horror house and may get eaten by a monster any day now, and all you can do is laugh."

"Oh yeah, I take anything seriously that threatens you. It's just that I don't see too much to worry about. If there's someone prowling around at two in the morning, it's probably because they don't want to be seen. They're not going to bother anyone. Most likely hoping no one bothers them, either. Now you better let me get back to work so we can get this done before the snow flies."

When Joey and Jamie came after school, they were chatting non-stop about the field trip their class was going on.

"We get to take our lunch and have a picnic out in the woods," Joey said.

"Yeah, and we get to find all kinds of leaves and stuff and make a book," Jamie added.

"That sounds like fun. When are you going?" Essie asked.

"Next Tuesday, but we gotta get a note saying we can go first, but Joey don't have to get one, cause his dad's the teacher." Jamie pulled out the note explaining the trip and showed it to Essie.

"I'm excited for you." She clapped her hands, remembering what a thrill it was for any little extra activity in elementary school.

"Yeah, we're excited for us, too." They giggled.

On Monday, Pete asked Essie if she would be home later that day. The painter had been contacted, and they would be coming by to talk to her. He, unfortunately, had to be out of town on business and wanted to know if he should reschedule the appointment.

"No, you know how anxious I am to get started. I can oversee it."

"Okay then. His name is Jim. He's a prince of a guy. He'll work with you on everything and give you his best price. If you have questions, just ask."

"Thank you for setting this up for me. I really appreciate it." She gave him a hug.

When Jim arrived, he and his men went through all the rooms she wanted painted along with the wallpapering. Then they went outside, measuring, counting windows and doors, and calculating all the things she wanted done. He gave her what she thought was a fair estimate. She accepted it, and Jim told her an approximate date he would start.

A few minutes after the painters left, Lark stopped in. The same exhilaration she always felt when he was around tugged at her brain.

"I have a dilemma," he told her.

"Oh no, I hate those things." She clapped her hand over her mouth. "Tell me, does it hurt?"

"No, not too much." He laughed. "I'm taking the class on a field trip tomorrow, and I need another chaperone. One of the parents canceled on me at the last minute. I was wondering if you could possibly go?" He put his hands together in mock prayer and waited for her to say something.

"The boys told me all about the trip. It sounds like fun. I'd be glad to go." She hoped she hadn't sounded too eager.

He breathed a big sigh. "Thank you. Maggie Randolph is going, but I don't think the two of us could handle twenty energetic kids out in the woods for three hours."

"I hear everyone's taking a picnic lunch." She smiled. "The boys tell me everything, so don't think you can keep secrets from me."

"Yes, we'll leave the school at ten, eat lunch at twelve, and be back about one." He chuckled. "And thanks for the warning."

"Sounds like you have it planned pretty good."

"We'll see. Second graders don't always stick to a plan. I'll see you at ten. And thank you. I owe you one." He turned to go.

"I'll be sure to collect." She caught her breath and held it momentarily. Flirting had never been her thing.

When she got to the school the next day, Lark and the other lady had begun loading the class onto the bus. He introduced her to Maggie as she helped the children buckle their seatbelts and encouraged them to hang on to their lunches. Joey and Jamie spotted Essie right away and ran to her to give her a hug.

"I'm so glad you get to go with us. Did you bring your lunch? We get to have a picnic at lunch. You can eat with me and Joey, since you know us." Jamie beamed proudly.

She chuckled. "You better go get on the bus, or you'll get left behind." They ran to the bus, and Maggie helped them get settled in.

"I understand you don't have kids in the school. Thanks so much for helping us," Maggie said as they took their seat together.

"I'm more than glad to help. What a nice day. And I love kids. I think I'm as excited as they are."

Lark stood in front and clapped his hands. "I want you to pay close attention. When we get there, I want you to get off the bus and wait for instructions. I also want you to partner up in twos or threes and don't ever lose track of each other. This is important. Remember, stay with the group and don't wander off by yourself. Do all of you understand?"

"Yes, Mr. Winters," they answered simultaneously.

When he sat, the bus driver closed the door. "Everybody got their seat belts on?" the driver asked.

"Yes, sir," they all shouted.

"Okay, off to see the wizard," the driver sang happily.

They drove about two miles to a small park, and the children filed off the bus and waited for Lark's instructions. A beautiful scene stretched out before them. The breeze blew gently as the last struggling leaves clung to their branches before letting go and fluttering softly to the ground to join the pile of bright red, yellow, and orange colors.

"What a perfect place for leaf hunting," Essie said to Maggie.

The children started gathering their leaves, exclaiming at each new find, and showing them off to their buddies. Maggie, Lark, and Essie watched them closely as they scurried among the brightly colored leaves, tossing them at each other and disappearing into the piles as they fell and were covered by their classmates.

"How innocent they are," Essie said to Lark and Maggie.

"I know, and how I wish we could keep them that way forever," Maggie said.

"Okay, you two. I'll see how innocent you think they are in fifteen minutes," Lark warned.

More and more, Essie began to see that playful, jovial side of Lark, and she had to admit she liked it.

A small girl, her pigtails covered with leaves, ran up to Maggie. "Mommy, Mommy, Beth and I have to go."

"Okay, I'll go with you. It's right this way." Maggie pointed to the path that led into the trees.

Lark leaned against a tree, his hands behind him. "So, what

do you think of our field trip?"

"I wouldn't have missed it for anything. The children are just precious." Essie drew in a big breath of the fresh air. "And it's so beautiful out here. We didn't have all these colors in Tulsa. Leaves mostly turned brown and fell."

"You really do like kids, don't you?" he asked seriously.

"I do. I guess that's because I'm still a kid at heart." She spread her hands toward the children. "Just look at them. It takes so little to make them happy. Us adults could take a lesson from them."

He looked her straight in the eyes. "Don't ever change." He hesitated a moment. "Essie, would you go to dinner with me sometime?"

She could feel her heart racing. "You mean like a date?"

He continued to stare at her. "Yes, I mean like a date."

"I'd like that." Her knees felt weak, and the pounding in her chest intensified.

"And Pete won't mind?" he asked. "I know you spend a lot of time with him. I don't want to cause any trouble."

"No, Pete and I aren't . . . it's not like that with us," she assured him. "But what about Diana? Won't she have something to say about me going out with you?" With her heart pounding, she waited anxiously for his answer.

"No, I'm not asking her to come along. It's just the two of us." He grinned.

They were interrupted as Maggie and the girls emerged from the trees. "I think it's about time for lunch if you want to get these kids back by one o'clock."

Lark looked at his watch. "You're right. My, how time flies when you're having fun." He winked at Essie. He put his fingers to his mouth and whistled. "Listen up. Go to the bus and get your lunches. Then come back out and find a grassy spot and sit down and eat. You have plenty time, so just enjoy your picnic."

The kids scampered off to the bus and grabbed their lunches. Joey ran up to Essie. "Come eat with us, please, Miss Essie."

She looked at Lark with a *what do I do?* look on her face.

"Joey, you go eat with the rest of your class. Mrs. Randolph and Miss Essie and I are going to eat right here at the table where we can watch everyone."

Joey walked off with a pout on his face. Lark and Essie looked at each other and burst out laughing.

Counting each child as they loaded the bus, Lark rechecked his list. Essie's admiration for him grew when she saw his deep dedication as a teacher and his care for the safety of the children.

When they got back to school, Lark thanked Maggie and Essie, then lined the kids up to march back into school.

Essie waved to Lark as she drove off. She smiled to herself, and her heart felt warm and tender inside her chest at the prospect of a date with him. So she'd been right about Lark thinking something was going on between her and Pete. But his answer when she asked about Diana had left her with a nagging feeling in the pit of her stomach.

At about five in the morning, Essie was startled awake when the phone rang. Her neck and shoulder muscles tensed as she stumbled out of bed and groped for her cell. When she picked up the phone and heard Lark's voice, she began to shake. Totally transferred back into time when she got the call about her parent's accident, she felt the chills run up and down her spine. Nothing good could come from a phone call this time of the morning.

"I'm sorry to wake you so early, but we have sort of an emergency. Miss Ida Belle is sick, and I'm taking her to the hospital." His voice sounded stressed. "I need someone to keep Joey and Jamie."

"Of course. Do you need me to come get them? Or do you need help with Miss Ida?" Still half asleep, her mind was fluttering between reality and imagination.

"No, I think I've got everything together that she'll need. I'll wake the boys and drop them off as soon as I can get them going."

"Is Miss Ida going to be okay? Do you know what's wrong?" She needed to hear some assurance from him.

"She doesn't want to go, but I'm insisting on it." He sounded tired and worried.

"I'll be waiting. I'll help them get ready for school. Don't worry about the boys. Just get Miss Ida the help she needs."

"Good. I should be back in time to take them to school. I really appreciate this."

"Don't mention it. I'm glad to help. Let me know if there's anything else I can do."

Essie waited on the porch until they arrived, and she and Lark took the two sleepy boys and put them in her spare bedroom. Lark was dressed in a blue cotton shirt and jeans. The shirt was wrinkled, his eyes dark from the lack of sleep, and a stubble of beard was just beginning to form.

"You look awful. How long have you been up?" she asked.

"Jamie called last night before he went to bed. I've told him before to call if he thinks his grandma needs help. He's such a little trooper. I took Joey and drove over to check on her. She didn't look too good, so I put the boys to bed and stayed there with her."

"I wish you'd called. I could have helped. Can you get her in the vehicle, okay?"

"I'm taking her car since it'll be easier than my truck to get her in. Don't worry about the boys, even if they miss a day at school."

"I won't. It'll be no problem getting them to school, but let me know what's going on."

"I will. I'll call if I can't make it. I'm thinking they'll keep her until they find out what's wrong."

"Is she in pain?"

"Not a lot, but there's something about how she looks. I just know she needs help."

"You'd better get back. Is she alone now?"

"Her neighbor's with her, but I do need to go. Thanks again. I'll let you know."

Lark returned from the hospital before eight o'clock. Essie had the boys up, dressed, and eating breakfast.

"How is she?" Essie asked, her voice trembling as she spoke.

"The doctor's keeping her until they can determine what's wrong. She hasn't been feeling well for a while. Naturally, she's worried about what will happen to Jamie while she's gone."

"Tell her not to. He can stay here with me until she's feeling better. I'll love having him. Or better yet, I'll go see her. She doesn't need that worry on top of everything else."

Lark was worried about Miss Ida. Wiping his hand across his forehead, he let out a big sigh. He'd known her since he came to Rosepoint. Establishing herself as a pillar of the community, she'd proven herself as the thread that held the town together. But more importantly, she was all the family Jamie had. Lark loved that little boy, as he did all his students, but he had a special place in his heart for Jamie. He was Joey's best friend, and the thought of him ending up in a strange place was beyond his imagination.

The elation he felt after Essie agreed to go on a date with him became second fiddle to Miss Ida. It would take him some time to figure out a way to handle the *Diana situation*.

He shook his head silently and took a big breath of fresh air. He'd given his word to her, and he wasn't about to break his promise, but somehow, he needed to let Essie know the truth of their relationship without affecting Diana's trust in him.

CHAPTER FIVE

Jamie kept watching out the window for Joey. Essie's promise to let him stay over on a school night went against her better judgment, but her heart went out to him when she thought of Miss Ida. When he saw Lark's truck pull up, he tore out the door to meet his best friend whom he'd seen only two hours before.

Essie watched out the window as Lark gathered Joey's things and followed the boys inside. "I hope you won't regret this," he said. "You have more nerve than I do."

She laughed. "I think I can survive one night. Besides, they're so adorable."

"Don't let them keep you awake all night with their chattering."

"I'll be fine. We'll have fun. Just go and have a free night to do whatever you want." She showed him out the door.

"Before you go upstairs, what would you like for supper?" she asked the boys as they headed up to the room where Jamie was staying.

Their eyes lit up as they looked at each other. "Pizza," they both hollered. "Please, Miss Essie, can we?" Jamie begged.

Essie's lips parted in a broad smile. "I should have known," she said. "Yes, you can have pizza. You go play for a while, and I'll order."

As they drove to Uncle Ziggy's, Essie experienced a feeling of deep satisfaction that she could help Miss Ida in her small way by giving Jamie a place to stay. The two buddies in the back seat chatting away, reminded her of the numerous times she and her pal, Emma, spent being utterly silly, but just being together was enough.

Essie left the boys in the car and hurried in to pick up the pizza. It was crowded and noisy, and as she looked around in a dark, secluded corner, she saw Lark and Diana in what appeared to be a serious conversation. She stepped further back behind the wall separating the bar and dining room, just enough so she could see, yet not enough to be seen. She watched as Lark let go of Diana's hand, walked around the table, took her in his arms, and kissed her.

Her heart beat rapidly, and her ears were ringing, but she didn't take her eyes off them as she waited for her order. She paid her bill and turned away from the man who'd captured her heart, trying hard to control the flood of tears that were about to erupt.

Essie tried desperately to control her emotions until the boys were in bed. As she thought about the situation, she realized she'd made this possible. Lark certainly knew how to use his free evening. And she certainly knew how to choose the wrong guy to fall for. She felt thankful for one thing, though, that kiss had cleared up a lot of things in her confused mind.

At seven o'clock the next morning, Essie heard her doorbell just as she woke the boys. When she went to answer it and saw Lark standing there, her heartbeat went from the old familiar pounding to a slow pang of disappointment as she remembered Diana wrapped in his arms.

"I know I'm too early to pick the boys up, but I know how slow Joey is in the morning. I thought I could come by and give him a little nudge, if you don't mind."

She gazed at him, then gave her head a side nod toward the parlor. "Would you like a cup of coffee?" she asked solemnly.

"No thanks, I've had my share already."

"The boys haven't eaten breakfast yet," she said as she reached for the cereal box. She filled the bowls with *Cheerios*, poured milk into each bowl, and set them in front of the boys. "And when you finish, go get your backpacks. You don't want to keep your dad waiting," she said to Joey.

As the boys finished eating and ran upstairs, Lark came around the table and leaned against the counter. He watched as she cleared the boys' bowls and put the cereal away.

"How did it go last night?" he asked. "Did the little chitter-chatters keep you awake all night?"

As she thought of the two little chatterboxes, she pushed away the smile that wanted to come from her lips. "They were fine. Naturally, they wanted Uncle Ziggy's for supper." She watched his face and waited for him to speak. She thought she could see a tiny bit of coloring pass through his cheeks.

He hesitated a moment, then stepped forward as Joey came down the steps. "Did you brush your teeth, bud?"

"I forgot."

"Go do it now, and don't dally." He looked at Essie and shook his head. "You see what I mean."

Joey, still standing in the same spot, giggled. "Does dally mean don't get my clothes messed up? You always tell me that."

"It means don't waste time. Oh yeah, Joey, don't get your clothes messed up."

"Daddy! You're so funny" He turned and ran back up the stairs.

As Essie listened to the conversation between father and son, a warm feeling ran through her whole body. What a lucky lady Diana is, she thought

Joey came back down the stairs, wiping his sleeve across his mouth.

Lark took a deep breath, shook his head, and smirked.

"Joey, what did I just tell you?"

"To not mess up my clothes. Oh!" He grabbed his shirt sleeve and rubbed his hand across it. "I forgot."

"You're awful forgetful this morning. Get your coat on. We need to go."

Joey grabbed his coat, and a folded paper fell to the floor. Lark bent to pick it up. "What have we here?" he asked as he unfolded it.

"It's a pictured I drawed in art. I was s'pose to give it to you, but I forg . . ."

Lark grinned. "But you forgot," he finished for him.

Joey slapped himself across the forehead. "I don't know why I keep saying that."

"I don't suppose that good-looking green dude with the big ears is me, huh?"

Joey fell back on the couch, giggling. "No, that's the green giant. Daddy, you're so silly."

When Lark got to school, the boys went to play with their classmates. Lark felt a lump in his throat. He wondered if he'd messed things up with Essie. With Joey gone last evening, he'd felt it a good time to discuss things with Diana. He picked her up, and they went to Uncle Ziggy's for pizza. He'd begun the conversation by asking her how she was.

"I'm fine," she answered casually.

"No, I mean, how are you, really?" Lark continued, feeling nervous because he didn't know quite how to bring up the subject without hurting Diana.

She looked at him funny. "Lark, is something wrong? What are you trying to say?"

"I guess what I'm trying to say is that you're a strong person, and I think you should start standing up for yourself. I think you've let yourself come to depend on my presence too much."

Her mouth stretched wide open. "Lark Winters, are you breaking up with me?"

"That's just it, Diana, there is no us. I think you knew that." He fiddled nervously with his hands, and his eyes pleaded for her to understand. "We'll always be friends, and you know I'll be there for you whenever you need me. It's not like we won't see each other every day at school."

Diana reached for Lark's hand. "I know you're right. I do need to start taking care of my own problems. I really appreciate all you have done for me. It's just that I'll really miss you."

"It's not like that. We can still do things together. And don't worry, your secret is safe with me. As far as anyone knows, we just decided to be friends instead of lovers." He grinned at her.

"Some lovers," she said. "I can truly say this is the longest relationship I've ever had without even a kiss."

"Then we better fix that," he said, getting up and going around the table. He took her in his arms and gave her a big kiss directly on the lips.

As he let her go, Lark gazed at Diana with an odd look. "Diana, you don't have feelings for me that way, do you."

She put her hand over her mouth, giggling. "I have to admit, I did have a small crush on you when we first started hanging out together, but sorry to burst your bubble, that kiss didn't do a thing for me." She grinned at him.

"Boy, now I'm hurt," Lark teased.

Lark let out a big sigh of relief, knowing things were going to be okay between him and Diana, but Essie had informed him she was there at Uncle Ziggy's last evening. Had she seen him kiss Diana?

Essie and Pete were off to see Miss Ida at the hospital shortly after Lark and the boys left for school. Sitting on the side of the bed with a nurse's aide braiding her hair, Essie fought to control her emotions as they entered her room.

Pete bent and kissed Miss Ida on the cheek. "How's the most beautiful girl in Rosepoint doing?"

Essie felt a lump in her throat as she saw the once vibrant little lady, usually dressed like a grand dame, sitting slumped over in a hospital gown, yet doing all she could to preserve her dignity and pretend all was well with her.

"You're so full of baloney, Peter. You sit down over there and behave yourself. Let this beautiful girl give me a hug." She held out her arms to Essie, who was waiting for Pete to move aside.

The aide patted Miss Ida on the shoulder and slipped out of the room.

Essie sat beside her and wrapped her arms around her. Delighted to see her still sassy and perky, she was encouraged somewhat but still couldn't erase the awful scenarios that had been running rampant in her mind.

"Tell me what's been going on out there while I've been stuck in this bed. How's my grandson doing?" She looked pointedly at Essie.

"Jamie's fine. He sends his love."

"I can't tell you what that little red-headed rascal means to me. I hope he's being good. I want to thank you for all you are doing." She picked up Essie's hand and squeezed it.

"You don't have to thank me. I'm enjoying every minute of it. He's such a precious little boy and no trouble at all."

She looked at Pete with a scowl on her face. "And you, young man, are you helping her, or are you too busy mowing all the pretty ladies' yards?"

He grinned. "Yes, ma'am, I'm doing both."

She pointed her finger at Pete. "You know that guy right

there takes care of all of us helpless females in Rosepoint?" She looked at him with tenderness.

"Yes, I do. Now tell me how you're doing? You gave everyone quite a scare," Essie said.

"Aw! Just an old lady's way of getting a little attention. I'll be fine," she said, giving a dismissive gesture with her hand.

"Is there anything else I can do, like watering your plants?"

"No, honey, I don't have any of those things. I always figured they were made to plant outside to aggravate men mowing your yard."

"Mission accomplished!" Pete laughed. "Miss Ida has the contents of a greenhouse scattered around her front lawn. At least an extra hour of mowing."

"One way of keeping you around longer. An old woman gets lonely."

"When do you think you can go home?" Pete stood and walked toward her bed.

"No one tells me anything. Quite frankly, I'm beginning to think that cute little doctor has a thing for me. He wants to keep me around longer." She winked at Pete.

He took both her hands in his. "Now, don't you go flirting with those doctors, Miss Ida. You'll make me jealous." He bent and gave her a kiss on the cheek.

"And I'll bring Jamie to see you this weekend if you aren't home by then." Essie gave her a hug, and Pete turned at the door and waved.

"She's such a brave lady," Essie said as they walked down the hall.

Pete shook his head. "I don't think she's as brave as she's pretending to be. I think she's thinking of Jamie and what might happen to him if she doesn't get better, but as usual, she's hiding behind that happy personality."

"What will happen to him?" Essie fought the lump that was forming in her throat.

"That's a good question, but unfortunately, with a bad answer. If there's no one else, he'll be put into the system."

"Oh no! We can't let that happen," she proclaimed loudly, panic spreading through her whole body.

Unable to sit still on the way home, she twisted and turned until Pete asked her if she was all right. All she could think of was Jamie in an orphanage, Jamie in a foster home, torn away from his buddy, Joey, or being mistreated by someone who was fostering strictly for the money. She made a promise to pray for Miss Ida, and to talk to her about Jamie.

Early the next morning, Pete arrived at the house with his tools, ready to finish the upstairs bath. Miss Ida had just called and said she was being released tomorrow, but only if she found someone to stay with her. She'd asked Pete to help her find a caretaker.

"It'll cost a fortune. I don't know how Miss Ida is financially, but I'd hate to see her spend all her money on nurses. I don't know what to do. And what about Jamie?"

Essie could see the worry on Pete's face. "Jamie's fine where he is," Essie said. "And why can't Miss Ida come here? We can move a bed down in the parlor so she won't have to climb the stairs."

"Whoa!" He threw his hands up in the air. "That's a big responsibility. It's not your place to solve all the world's problems."

"But it *is* the perfect solution." Essie scanned the room, planning the setup of the room in her head. "The painters aren't coming for a couple of weeks. By that time, she should be able to go home, or if she isn't, we'll decide what to do then. This way, she can be together with Jamie, and I'll be cooking anyway, so it won't be that much more trouble."

"She's a proud lady. I don't think she'll agree to that. She'll think of it as an imposition."

"We'll just have to talk her into it," Essie said with finality.

"Oh, I forgot to tell you, there's another meeting scheduled about the community hall. Matt admitted the rumors were true. He wouldn't bend one inch. His intentions are to start renovations in about three months."

"Nice fellow, sad to know he thinks the town needs a supper club more than a community hall. So, is there anything else we can do about it?" Essie had never met this Matt guy, but she was forming an opinion about him, and it wasn't a good one.

"Probably not, if he has his mind made up. Kind of like somebody else I know." He winked at her and chuckled.

"I won't be going to the meeting because I'll have house guests." She grinned. "Now, we better get busy moving that bed."

"Don't you think you should talk to her first?" Pete asked.

"What choice does she have? Either come here or stay at the hospital." She grabbed the side table and moved it against the wall.

Watching her clear the space for the bed, Pete slid the old wooden rocker out of the way. "I would hate to be on the opposite end of your determination. Woe to the poor fellow who marries you."

"Ha, ha." She made an ugly face at him.

"I'll ask Lark to help me move the mattress when he drops Jamie off."

The image of Lark kissing Diana flashed through her mind. She turned away. "We don't need to bother him. I can help you."

"Not this time, Essie, the mattress is too heavy for you. I insist."

When Lark stopped to let Jamie off, Essie was waiting for him. "You and Joey, come inside. Lark and I need to talk to you, and Pete needs a little help from you."

"I hope all's well with Miss Ida." She could see the worry on his face. "She seemed better when I was there yesterday."

"She's being released tomorrow. That's what we wanted to talk to you about." She opened the door, and Lark followed her inside.

"Can you wait just a minute while I give the boys a snack?" She went to the cookie jar, the colorful little clown smiling his goofy grin at her, and one so familiar to her from her childhood. She took out two cookies each, poured them a glass of milk, and sent them out to the clubhouse.

Lark leaned against the door, watching her. "How are things going with Jamie? Kind of interrupts your peace and quiet, doesn't it?" He chuckled.

"It certainly livens things up a bit. Let's go sit. Pete and I want to talk to you."

He followed her into the parlor where Pete waited. "Miss Ida is coming home, but she can't be alone. Essie has the bright idea that she should stay here with her until she's able to go home." He waited for Lark's reaction.

He looked at Pete, then over at Essie. "And what does Miss Ida say?"

"We haven't discussed it with her. She wanted me to find someone to stay with her at her house," Pete said.

"That might be impossible to do in a small town like this," Lark said.

"I'm afraid you're right. You know Miss Ida pretty well. Do you think she would agree to coming here?" Essie asked.

"Maybe, if it would keep her out of the hospital. How long before she could go home?"

"We don't know. It'll depend on how long it takes to regain her strength," Essie replied.

"Essie wants to put a bed in this room. I can put it together again, but I need some extra muscle to help move it from upstairs," Pete said.

Lark flexed his muscles. "Let's go do it," he said with a grin.

As the men wrestled the heavy mattress down the stairs, Essie went to talk to the boys.

"Jamie, I have a surprise for you. Your grandmother's coming home tomorrow."

His face lit up. "I'm glad she's all well again. I don't like it when my grandma's sick." He looked at her with a solemn expression. "Does that mean I have to go back home?"

"Maybe not. Your grandmother needs someone to take care of her for a while. So if it's all right with her, both of you will be staying here with me until she feels better."

"Yeah!" He broke into a big grin, jumping up and down.

Lark was helping Pete put the bed back together again, so she went into the kitchen and threw together a hamburger-macaroni casserole. It was one of her favorites and the least she could do for the two men who probably survived on pizza and sandwiches. It would be a good healthy meal for the boys.

As they sat down to eat, Essie said to Lark, "Pete tells me there was no progress made on the community hall. Do you think there's anything to be done that can stop this Matt guy?"

Lark shook his head. "I don't know what. Kind of looks like our hands are tied."

"What about it being too close to the school? Isn't there some ordinance against it?"

"Of course we will look into that. The only other thing I can think of is a petition. Maybe play a little on his compassion, that is, if he has any."

"Rumors have it, he's a pretty tough fellow to break," Pete said. "Once he sets his mind to accomplish something, he does it."

"We have a meeting at the mayor's house tomorrow evening. Hopefully, we can come up with something," Lark said.

"Well, I'm going home to get some rest," Pete said. "This woman drives me day and night." He blew out a big breath of air. "A slave driver if I ever saw one."

Essie slapped him on the back. "Get out of here, you worthless scalawag."

"Are you sure you're up to having Miss Ida stay here? Jamie's one thing, but she's going to need a lot of attention," Lark asked after Pete left.

"I know it won't be easy, but it's something that needs to be done, and I have the room and the time. I really want to do this for Miss Ida."

Lark took Essie's hands, and his eyes held hers. "Do you know what an asset you are to this community?"

Her heart leaped at the touch of his fingers on hers. "I just happen to have a big house and a lot of time. I like Miss Ida, and I love having Jamie here."

He continued to hold her hands. "It's about time we had that dinner date we talked about. How about it?"

She thought about Diana and the kiss she saw him give her. Her heart wanted to say yes, but her common sense told her something very wrong was going on. "I think I'll have my hands full for a while," she answered.

"You won't have to do this all alone. She has lots of friends that will help out. And you know, I'll do anything I can to help." He gave her a kiss on the cheek and squeezed her hands. "I'm going to get Joey and go home. I'll see you tomorrow after school and help get your patient settled in."

Miss Ida called shortly before noon, and Pete and Essie stopped at a rental place and got a wheelchair on the way to the hospital. Asking about her caregiver when she called, Pete told her it was taken care of, and he would explain it all when he got there. The nurse had just finished her paperwork, and Miss Ida was anxiously awaiting their arrival.

She greeted them with a smile. "My heroes are here, coming to take me away from this life of boredom, back into civilization. Come here and give me a hug, you two." She held out her arms. "Now tell me, who did you find that can put up with a cranky old woman like me?"

Essie spoke up. "You're coming home with me, and you are not a cranky old woman, so you just stop that."

Her eye caught Pete's gaze, then Essie's. She shook her head. "Oh no, sweetie, you can't do that. I won't be a burden to anyone. You've done enough already."

"You're not a burden," Essie said. "I'll love having you, and since Jamie's already there, it'll give you some time together. It's the perfect solution."

"No, it's not." Miss Ida shook her head violently. "There must be someone who will come to my house." She looked at Pete. "Did you try to find anyone, or are you two plotting against me?"

Pete shrugged. "She's a determined woman."

"Miss Ida, we already have a room fixed for you. It'll work out. You'll see."

"I guess I have no choice. I'll do anything to get out of here, but I'll find a way. I'm not going to do this to you," Miss Ida said.

Essie patted her shoulder. "Let's get you in the wheelchair, and I'll load your flowers on this cart."

Pete gently helped Miss Ida into the chair and went to get the nurse. Essie listened as the nurse gave her instructions. Then they rolled her to the car and loaded her in.

They went directly to Miss Ida's house, wheeled her inside, put together a suitcase full of things she might need, and drove to Essie's house.

They wheeled her into the parlor. Beside the bed, Essie had moved the small table back and supplied it with all the necessary things she thought Miss Ida might need.

"Oh my goodness, honey child, what have you done?" Tears came to Miss Ida's eyes. "You've torn your house apart for me."

Essie patted her on the back. "All I've done is move a bed. Pete and Lark did that last night. We just want to make you comfortable."

"You have certainly done that." She swiped at the tear as it trickled down her cheek.

Pete rolled Miss Ida over by the bed. "I'm going to help you into bed, and you can take a nice long nap. I'm sure all this commotion has tired you out."

When Essie got Miss Ida settled, she closed the door and went to join Pete on the back porch. "That went over a lot easier than I thought. She must really be wiped out."

"Yes, I think that ride took a lot more out of her than we realized. She'll get her fighting spirit back as soon as she is rested."

Essie chuckled. "I'm sure you're right about that."

"Grandma," Jamie squealed as he ran to give her a hug when he got home. "I missed you so much. I'm glad you don't have to be in that hospital no more. I don't like it when you're sick." He chatted non-stop, telling her all that had happened since she'd been gone. Lark stopped by briefly to say hello but had to get ready for the meeting at the mayor's office.

"Leave Joey here with Jamie. You can pick him up after the meeting," Essie said.

He shook his head. "What Miss Ida doesn't need is another chatty little mouth around right now. I'm dropping him off at Mrs. Pearson's. He needs to be with her occasionally. I don't want them to lose touch."

It was a school night, so Jamie went to bed early. As soon as Essie got him tucked in, she went to join Miss Ida. "I'm sorry you can't be at home like you wanted, but at least we'll know you're being taken care of properly."

"Honey, I owe you a lot. How can I ever repay you?" She paused, looking at Essie with admiration in her eyes.

"You don't owe me anything," Essie assured her. "We all just want you well again."

"I'm an old woman, Essie, and I'm not dumb. I know it's all downhill from here." She took a tissue from the box on the table. "Let's be honest, I don't want to die, but I've lived a good life, and I know I'm headed to a better place. That's not the problem. It's all about Jamie now."

Essie could feel her muscles tensing. Did she know more about herself than she'd told them? "Tell me about your illness. What did the doctor say was causing you to have these episodes?"

"It's got some fancy name, but what it comes down to is some kind of bug that got into my bloodstream, and they can't seem to get rid of it."

"They're finding new cures every day. Don't you dare give up," Essie scolded her.

"My mind's willing, but this old body ain't got much fight left in it. I can't quit worrying about Jamie." Miss Ida wiped away a tear as it rolled down her cheek. "What will happen to him if I don't make it?"

Essie pulled herself upright, put a smile on her face, and took Miss Ida's hand. "Miss Ida, don't talk like that. You're going to be around for a long time."

"You don't know that. Let's face facts. I'm old, and I'm sick. Maybe I was being selfish when I adopted Jamie, but I couldn't see him going into a stranger's home. He was my only grandchild."

"You weren't being selfish. You've given him a good, loving home."

"Lord knows, I've tried." Miss Ida's shoulders slumped as she talked to Essie.

Essie's heart broke listening to the defeat in her voice. "I'm not trying to pry, but is there any chance either of his parents might take him?" Essie asked cautiously.

"Not a chance. His mother never wanted him, and my son, God rest his soul, can't even take care of himself."

Trying to hold back the tears, Essie felt the burning behind her eyes as she walked to the window and stared outside. Evidence of fall was all around. The last of the bright-colored leaves were torn from their branches and tossed about by gusts of chilly wind, reminding her of the cold winter ahead. She thought of Jamie helping Pete rake. She thought of the field trip they took and of Jamie jumping in the leaves with his buddy, Joey. She would never let him be torn away from the ones he loved.

She walked back to the bed and took Miss Ida's hand. "I'll make you a promise. Jamie will never go into the system, so I want you to stop worrying and just concentrate on getting well."

Essie felt a warmness run through her body as she saw the relief in Miss Ida's eyes. There was one thing that was clear in her mind, she'd made this promise, and she intended to keep it.

When Lark stopped by the next evening to see Miss Ida, Essie peeked in to see if she was sleeping. She opened her eyes and winked at her. "Some more of my fan club here to see me?" she asked.

Lark laughed. "One of your biggest fans, Miss Ida."

"Sorry, no more autographs today. My hand is worn out."

He pulled a chair up beside her bed, took her hand, and Essie left them happily chatting as she slipped out of the room.

As the boys came down from Jamie's room, Essie could hear Miss Ida calling them.

When she turned around, Lark stood there watching her, his arms folded as he leaned his tall frame against the doorway. "Your patient looks like she's doing good. Speaks well for her nurse."

Essie laughed. "I'm afraid my nursing skills are very limited."

"Do you need anything? Can I help in any way?" he asked earnestly.

"We're doing fine. Her biggest worry is about what will happen to Jamie if she can no longer take care of him."

"I know." He lowered his voice. "I've thought about that also. Did she say if she had any arrangements made in case she was unable to do that anymore?"

"No, evidently, she doesn't. I've tried to reassure her. I mean it, Lark, I will not let that little boy go into the system."

"You can only do so much, Essie." He walked over to the table, pulled out a chair, and sat. "It's so sad. We'll just have to hope she gets over this infection, or whatever it is."

She could see the compassion in his eyes as she sat down beside him. "I hope so, too. Now tell me what happened at the meeting last night?"

He shook his head. "The way it looks, there isn't much we can do if Matt doesn't change his mind."

"So is this the end of it?" She threw up her hands in dismay. "We're just going to lose our community hall? I can't believe there isn't something we can do."

"The mayor is looking into how close it is to the school, and two of the ladies are starting a petition . . . not that we think it will do any good."

"I guess all we can do is try." It was disheartening, but she had bigger things to worry about now.

Essie called Dee and made an appointment to come wash and set Miss Ida's hair. When she arrived, Essie took the opportunity to make a quick trip to the grocery store. As she was shopping for fresh produce, she saw Claire, Dee's sister-in-law, talking to Annie Coburn. Hearing the name Pete, she ducked around the corner where she couldn't be seen.

"There was no mistaking. It was him. It was on Monday, two weeks ago. I remember because that was the day before the kids' field trip. I was on my way to the store to get some things for Timmy's lunch. He and some creepy guy with long hair were sneaking around the Sawyer place. Looks like he didn't want to be seen. Looked real cozy to me, if you know what I mean. They sure ducked inside when they saw me looking."

"I've heard lots of talk about lights and odd things happening there. I just figured it was some rumor started by someone," Annie said. "You know how things spread once they get started."

"Well, this is no rumor. I saw him with my own eyes. I've wondered about that guy. He almost seems too good to be true. No one knows anything about him, not even where he's from. He doesn't work, yet he always has money. Makes me think he might be into dealing drugs or something. It's scary to think something like that's happening right here in our own town."

Essie slipped away and went to pay for her groceries. As she headed for her car, she thought about the conversation between the two ladies. She didn't believe it for a minute. Besides, Pete was at her house almost every day. Claire had mentioned Monday before the field trip. That was the day the painters were at her house. Pete had told her he was out of town that day. That would prove it couldn't have been him. But Claire seemed so sure it was him. Had he lied to her? But why?

CHAPTER SIX

After a week, Miss Ida was improving every day. She obviously felt anxious to get back home, but Essie didn't think she was ready to be on her own. She especially didn't think she was ready to care for Jamie.

"Wait until you get a little more strength back. You know I would be running over to your house all the time, checking on you. It'll be a lot easier on both of us if you stay right here for now," Essie said.

"I know you're right, but you're spending all your time spoiling me. I'll never get my strength back if you're there with a wad of toilet paper every time I need to wipe my behind," Miss Ida said.

"Besides, you know your doctor will never agree to let you stay alone."

"John Morris? What does he know? I've been around twice as long as he has. I wiped his little butt when he was just a baby."

"You're too weak to even go to the bathroom without help. How would you manage?"

Miss Ida chuckled. "I guess that would be a bit messy, wouldn't it? Sort of looks like I have no choice but to stay a few more days, but only if you promise to quit coddling me."

"I guess it's in my nature to coddle," Essie said.

"You need to find yourself a man, young lady. Like that handsome schoolteacher that hangs around here all the time, pretending he's coming to see me."

"Now, Miss Ida, don't you go trying to fix me up. Lark isn't interested in me." Essie thought of Diana and the kiss she'd witnessed with her own eyes. There was no mistaking something like that.

Miss Ida's lips broke into a wide grin. "This old gal has been around the block a few times, and I say one look at that face when he's around you, and anyone can tell he's a goner."

"But he's going out with Diana Jordan. You know, the lady who's in charge of the plays."

"Take it from me," Miss Ida said. "I've seen a few of those looks before, and believe me, he's hooked."

When Lark dropped Jamie off after school, he asked Essie about Miss Ida.

"She's awake. Come say hello," she said, leading him into the parlor where Miss Ida sat propped up in bed playing a game of solitaire.

"You're looking much better," he said, bending down and giving her a kiss on the cheek. "Essie must be taking good care of you."

Miss Ida nodded her head, directing her eyes earnestly at Essie. "She's doing a wonderful job. I'll never be able to repay her. Not only for me, but for Jamie, too."

"You know I don't need any repayment. It's been a pleasure to have you both here." Essie turned to go. "I'll leave you two to visit while I go clean the kitchen." As she walked out, Essie heard something that made her stop and listen.

"What that girl needs is a break from looking at this old wrinkled face. Why don't you take her out for an evening of relaxation this weekend?"

"I'd love to do that, but you know she won't leave you alone here with just Jamie," Lark said.

"What do you think? I've got no friends? Any one of them will come over and stay with me for a few hours. Don't take no for an answer. That sweet girl needs some fun in her life."

"I'll do my best." Lark lifted his eyes upward. "Thank you, Jesus," he whispered as he stood to leave.

Essie's heart beat fast at the thought of a date with Lark as she retreated to the kitchen. She wondered if he would ask her, and if he did, would it only be because Miss Ida had asked him to.

"She's pretty perky today. What are you feeding her, any-way?" he asked, as he followed Essie back into the kitchen.

Essie laughed. "With Miss Ida, you don't need food to perk her up."

"Could I interest you in going to dinner with me on Satur-day?" He shifted to his other foot.

"Thank you for asking, but I can't leave her and Jamie here alone. She's not well enough yet."

He took her arms and gently turned her toward him. "No excuses. This is a direct order from Miss Ida. She said you needed to get away from her wrinkled face, is the way I be-lieve she put it."

"But I can't," she argued. "She's still so sick, and there's Jamie."

"She said she would call one of her friends," he insisted.

"It would be nice to get out, but how can I find someone I'd trust? And don't forget, there's Jamie, too. I'd never for-give myself if something happened to Miss Ida while I was gone."

"We'll find someone, so prepare yourself for a night of din-ing and dancing. I'll pick you up at six on Saturday. You do dance, don't you?"

"I love dancing, but it's been a long time since I've been on the floor." She pictured herself in his arms.

He grinned. "Should I wear steel-toed shoes?"

"Hopefully, I won't be that bad."

He touched his hand to her cheek. She felt her heart leap.

"I'm really looking forward to our date," he said.

On Saturday, Essie flitted around the house, singing and teasing Jamie, laughing with Miss Ida, and nervously occupying her time with whatever she could find to do. She stopped trying to hide her excitement from Miss Ida as they discussed what she should wear and how she should fix her hair. She tried on three different outfits, finally getting approval at last on a light green A-line, accented with a simple strand of pearls and matching teardrop earrings.

It had been arranged for Miss Ida's friend, Florence, to come visit, and at nine o'clock, Pete would give her a ride home and sit with Miss Ida until Essie and Lark returned. That way, they could stay as long as they liked. Jamie would spend the night with Joey at his house with their favorite babysitter.

When Lark arrived, Essie greeted him at the door. "Wow! You look gorgeous," he said.

"Thanks," Essie said, her heart fluttering as the smell of his aftershave filled the air. He held her coat for her.

Miss Ida called out from the parlor, "Of course she's gorgeous. I'm surprised you haven't noticed before. Now you two kids get out of here and go have some fun. Florence and I have a bunch of catching up to do."

They grinned at each other and shook their heads. "Goodnight, Miss Ida," they both echoed.

They drove to a place called Trevor's, about two miles from town. Not overly impressed with the outside of the restaurant, Essie drew in a quick breath as she took in the sight of the glamorous interior. The tables were appropriately placed at a distance from each other, befitting the subdued atmosphere in which the guests dined. On top of each sparkling white tablecloth was an array of beautiful china, each in its own unique pattern. Soft music played in the background as the diners enjoyed their meal in a leisurely manner. Lark gave the host his reservation information, and they were shown to their table.

He smiled at her. "You look surprised. Not exactly a fast-food joint, huh?"

"You're right. I am surprised." She realized that this was the one thing she missed about the city. It helped build a girl's self-confidence to be able to dress up and go out for a carefree evening. And deep down, she knew it was pride, but it didn't hurt to have an admiring glance once in a while from an uninvolved spectator.

"People drive from all the small towns around to eat here. It has quite a reputation," Lark explained.

"Is it locally owned? How did it come to be in a small town like Rosepoint?" Essie asked in awe.

"It's locally owned. It seems the young man went off to school, intending to establish his restaurant in a big city somewhere, but he was such a mama's boy he couldn't stand to be away, so he came back here and built. It's been here about fifteen years."

"Looks like it's worked well for him."

"It has. He's never regretted it, and neither have the locals. We're very fortunate to have a place like this, especially so close by. But he's worked hard to build a good reputation for this place."

"You sound like you know him well. Is he a friend of yours?"

Lark hesitated. "He's Diana's cousin. She sometimes helps out here on the weekends when they're real busy."

"Oh." Essie didn't know what else to say.

They placed their order. When the waitress set a sizzling steak before Lark, and Essie's favorite, battered shrimp, they ate heartily, both agreeing their food was delicious. They were offered dessert, which they declined.

"Thank you for bringing me here," Essie said. "I never would have imagined a place like this so close by." Suddenly realizing the tension in her shoulders had eased, she felt her whole body relaxing.

"Thank you for coming. I'm glad you enjoyed it. Would you like to go for a walk? It'll be a while before the band starts playing."

She patted her stomach. "I think that would be a good thing to do right now."

Lark paid their bill and got their coats. The air was a little nippy as they stepped outside.

"Winter's almost on us," Lark commented as they strolled along. "How's a girl from Oklahoma going to survive a Wisconsin winter, especially when it gets thirty below?"

"Probably by staying inside, mostly. I'm just hoping the painters get my house painted before it gets too cold."

As they strolled along, they came to a small park. Its winding walkways bordered a small stream of clear rippling water that coiled its way throughout the park. Beautiful maple and tall oak trees painted a picturesque backdrop to the now-fading flowers placed neatly along the way.

Lark casually reached for her hand and guided her toward a bench. "Do you know how long I've waited for this date?" He squeezed her hands. "I've wanted to ask you out since the first time I met you."

Essie's heart beat so hard she could hardly speak. "So why didn't you?" She listened to the sincerity in his speech and melted as the tenderness in his eyes took her beyond her fondest fantasy.

"I was afraid you would say no. I take rejection pretty hard." Lark reached up and let his hand gently slide down her cheek.

Essie felt her voice cracking at the touch of his hand. "Why do you think I would've said no?"

"I'm not sure, but by the time I got the nerve to ask you, Pete was always around."

"But I told you there was nothing going on between us," Essie quickly answered. "He's been a good friend, that's all."

"I know, but I didn't know that at the time." Lark grinned. "A man gets jealous when he sees another person in the picture."

Tell me about it, she thought. "Speaking of Pete . . ." She brushed a leaf out of her hair. "I heard something the other day that's hard for me to believe."

"Something about Pete? I can't imagine what, but then, he's a bit of a mystery."

"Yes," Essie said. "I was in the grocery store when I overheard Claire telling Annie Coburn that she'd seen Pete over at the Sawyer place with a suspicious-looking character."

"First off, coming from Claire, I wouldn't make too much of it. Did you ask Pete about it?"

"No, I wouldn't do that. I don't want to believe it, but the thing is, I realized Pete lied to me. He told me he was going out of town on business that day." She inhaled deeply and shook her head.

Lark put his arm around her and pulled her to him. "Are you sure it was the same day? And are you sure it was really Pete she saw?"

"I don't know, she sounded so sure. I know it was the same day because the painters were coming, and he was upset because he couldn't be there."

"Claire's known to, let's say, exaggerate sometimes. And Annie, she couldn't have told a worse person. She's known around town as our local newscaster," Lark said.

Essie sighed. "I feel so bad for Pete. They think he's dealing drugs or something. I don't believe that for a minute, yet I don't understand why he lied to me."

"I'm with you. Pete's a good guy. I've known him almost

since he came to town. If it was him she saw, I'm sure he had his reasons." Lark tightened his arm around Essie and squeezed her to him. "Should we get back and enjoy some music for a while? I'm sure you'll find out there's nothing to worry about."

When they returned, the band was tuning up. They found a table far enough away from the noise so they could talk, yet close enough to watch them play. Essie loved to dance. Amazingly, Brad never complained when they were dancing. They'd spent many evenings dancing into the wee hours of the night. The thought of being in Lark's arms brought her forgotten fantasy back to life once again.

He reached across the table and took her hand in his, then he pulled her up and out onto the dance floor, never taking his eyes off her. As she slipped into his arms, butterflies filled her heart. Her heart was beating wildly as he guided her around the floor, gently pulled her into a snuggle, and their cheeks rubbed softly against each other. When the music stopped and they pulled apart, her knees were weak.

On the way back to their table, they both spotted Diana in the far corner, talking to someone, yet staring intently at them. When Diana saw them looking her way, she turned away at once.

Lark seated Essie at the table and, putting his hand on her shoulder, he said, "I hope you understand. I have to go talk to her for just a minute. Will you be all right?"

Essie nodded her head, and Lark made his way through the crowd. Her heart skipped a beat, and she had a hollow feeling in the pit of her stomach as she watched him walk away. She watched every move they made. They talked for a few minutes, nodding at each other. Then Lark gave her a hug and started back to their table.

As Lark came toward her, Essie took a big breath, relaxed her shoulders, and shifted her gaze to the band. Was he still dating Diana? If so, what did Diana think of all this?

"Can I get you another drink?" Lark reached for the almost empty glass before her.

"No, I'm fine." She drank the last of her wine and set the glass aside.

He sat and reached for her hand. "Essie, I'm sorry. I needed to go say hello. She's a good friend and colleague."

Essie grinned. "I understand, but I feel like the villain in this situation." She watched for his reaction.

Lark rose, never letting go of her hand and pulled her toward the dance floor. "I hope so because villains are more my type," he said as he took her into his arms.

Essie snuggled into his arms like she belonged there. As they twirled across the floor to fast as well as slow tunes, it gave her the kind of joy she'd never imagined. They spoke little as their bodies moved in rhythm to the music, their cheeks touching, sending thrills into Essie's heart. They stayed until the band played their last tune.

Sighing heavily as Lark walked to his side of the truck to get in, Essie hated to see the night come to an end. As they drove home, she closed her eyes and felt herself in his arms, gliding over the dance floor. She could smell the sweet aroma of his body as he held her close. If only for a moment, she could forget Diana.

As they drove into the driveway and Lark turned the engine off, he pulled her closer to him.

Looking her straight in the eyes, he said, "I don't want to see this night end. I had a wonderful time."

"I know. I guess Miss Ida was right. I really did need to get away."

"Thank you, pretty lady, for going out with me," he whispered. Laying his hand on her cheek, he drew her to him, and their lips met.

She knew she was losing her heart to this handsome schoolteacher. Her knees were weak as she stepped out of the truck. Even the light touch of Lark's hand on her back as they walked to the door gave her goosebumps. She'd never felt this way before.

"We'll do this again soon," he said.

Miss Ida was asleep. True to Pete's promise, he'd come at nine o'clock, washed the dinner dishes, gave Florence a ride home, and got Miss Ida settled for the night. She marveled at his dependability and at the good friend he'd become to her. It had been a long time since she'd even thought about God, but tonight she would say a prayer of thanks for Pete and for this small town that had accepted her as one of their own.

Floating on a cloud, Lark returned to his truck for the short drive home. It had been his dream date, holding her in his arms and dancing the night away. Even the presence of Diana hadn't dampened the atmosphere. For a fleeting moment, he thought of Jane and Essie together and knew if the circumstances had been different, they would've been friends. He'd always hold a place in his heart for Jane, but he knew it was time for him to move on. He was falling head over heels for Essie.

The next morning Essie woke up early, and Miss Ida sat waiting for a full report on her evening out with Lark. When Essie asked her what she wanted for breakfast, she scowled at her. "Never mind my breakfast, young lady. You sit right down here and tell me all about your date with that handsome young man last night."

Essie's heart skipped when she thought of their kiss. "He took me to a place called Trevor's."

"Of course, it's the only place to go."

Essie went to the refrigerator and pulled out a carton of eggs. "We had a nice dinner. The food was delicious."

"Aw, come on, the food is always wonderful there. Let's get to the romantic part of the evening. Did you dance the evening away?"

"Yes, we danced. The band was very nice."

"You're going to make me drag it out of you, aren't you? Did you have a good time? Did he kiss you? Of course he kissed you. He'd be a fool not to."

Essie blushed. "It was just a date. We had a nice dinner and danced to a nice band. We even ran into Diana."

Miss Ida sighed. "That lady really bothers you, doesn't she? She seems to always turn up wherever you are."

"More like she turns up wherever Lark is."

"Did he ask you for another date?" Miss Ida asked.

"We didn't make a specific date, but he did say he wanted to go out again."

"Then, there you go. Good Lord, honey child, don't worry about that other woman. That man is crazy about you. Anyone can tell that by being in the same room with you two."

"But I saw him kissing her, and it wasn't just a peck on the cheek, either. He only took me out because you told him to." Essie took a big breath.

Miss Ida shook her head. "Well, I don't know what's going on, and excuse this old woman for meddling, but I can sure find out for you."

"No, Miss Ida, please don't say anything to him." Essie bent forward and placed her hand on Miss Ida's shoulder. "You've got to promise. This is something I have to figure out on my own."

"You're right, this is none of my business, but I hate to see him wasting all those kisses on the wrong woman."

"Diana is a nice lady, and beautiful, too. I can see how he

would be attracted to her, them both being teachers. They have a lot in common."

"Hogwash, you're just as pretty as she is. Has anyone ever told you those blue eyes of yours can delve right into a person's soul? It's about time you wipe out that sadness that's always lurking behind them." She grinned up at Essie with a touch of mischief in her eyes. "Besides, you bake the best chocolate chip cookies I've ever eaten."

Essie shook her head. "Chocolate chip cookies may satisfy one's appetite, but I doubt if it'll go very far in capturing one's heart."

Miss Ida looked at her intently. "Honey, you've really got it bad for that guy, haven't you?"

Essie cracked an egg into the pan, then turned to face Miss Ida. She tried hard to stop the flow of tears that were trying to push themselves forward.

"Try telling him how you feel. If he's dumb enough not to see it already, then you have to let him know."

"I can't do that. If he has feelings for Diana, I can't have a part in breaking them up. He's the one who has to decide who he wants to be with."

"All I can say is, fight for your man. I predict you two will end up together. Now, are you going to give me that egg, or are you going to cook it until it can be used for a hockey puck?"

Essie got Jamie ready for church and sent him down the street to Mrs. Dawson's, who had offered to give him a ride to Sunday school. She ate her breakfast, and while cleaning the kitchen, she thought she heard a moan from Miss Ida.

Essie hurried to her bedside and saw Miss Ida wreathing in pain, her small body pulled up into a fetal position. Quickly calling nine-one-one, she shuffled around to find Miss Ida's purse with her insurance information. Then she packed a small bag with her robe and a few items, never taking her eyes off her. With a sigh of relief, she heard the ambulance stop in front of her house and a knock on the door.

When they had Miss Ida loaded into the ambulance and drove out, Essie grabbed the purse and bag and jumped in her car to follow, shaking so badly she could hardly control the wheel. She realized she had to notify someone so that Jamie wouldn't be alone when he got home. But who? Everyone would be at church, and their phones would most likely be turned off. She pulled over to the side of the road and tried Pete and Lark, with no results. Pulling back onto the road, she made a mental note to keep track of the time and call them later.

When she got to the hospital, she parked, went inside, and gave the front desk the information they needed. She was told to wait in the front lounge.

Forty-five minutes later, she was still waiting. About the time for the church to dismiss, she called Pete's number, and he answered. After she told him what was going on, he told her that he would take care of everything, inform everyone, and be there as soon as he could. She was still waiting when Pete and Lark arrived.

"How is she?" they both asked at once.

"I haven't heard a thing since I was told to wait here," she said impatiently.

"I'll check," Lark said as he headed toward the desk.

Pete put his arm around Essie's shoulder. "And how are you doing?"

"I'm okay, just a little nervous."

"Can you tell me what happened?"

"She was fine. She ate an egg and toast and was talking and joking around. I was in the kitchen and heard her moaning. I could see she was in so much pain, I called nine-one-one right away."

He squeezed her to him. "You did the right thing. She's in good hands now."

They watched as Lark talked to the nurse. When he started their way, they went to meet him.

"I didn't find out much. The doctor is still with her, but they'll be settling her in a room soon, and they'll let us know."

The tears gathered in Essie's eyes. "She was in so much pain."

Lark reached out and touched her arm. "They've given her medicine to relieve that. She's pretty well out of it right now."

"That's okay. I would rather she be out than hurting the way she was. Where are the boys?" Essie asked.

"They went home with Mrs. Pearson. She said to not worry about them. They could even spend the night if it got too late, and she would get them to school tomorrow if necessary."

When the nurse came for them, she warned them that Miss Ida wouldn't be awake for a while, but they could sit with her if they wished. The three of them went to her room and sat quietly, watching for any movement from her.

When Essie saw Miss Ida stir, she went to her and held her hand. Miss Ida grimaced up at her with one eye closed.

"That must have been some powerful egg you gave me for breakfast," Miss Ida rasped out.

Essie smiled. "Now, don't you go blaming me for this, Miss Ida. You know that was a perfectly good egg."

They all gathered around her.

"You have to quit scaring us like this. We're not getting any younger, you know," Lark teased.

"Yes, cut the dramatics, Miss Ida. If you miss me so much, all you need to do is ask, and I'll be right over," Pete said as he bent and kissed her on the cheek. "Are you feeling better?"

"All I'm feeling now is sleepy." Her eyes closed, and she drifted back to sleep.

Lark nodded his head toward the door, and they both

followed him into the hall. "We need to find out from some-one what's going on with her. How bad is it, and does some-one need to be here with her? Do we need to try to locate her son?"

"I'll go talk to the nurse to see if the doctor can talk to us," Pete said. He headed for the nurse's station.

"Do you have any idea how to locate her son?" Essie asked.

Lark shook his head. "No, in fact, I don't know if she even knows where he is, but I know someone who can try to locate him for us. It may take some time, so I'll get on it right away."

"Why don't we just ask her? Or is that not a good idea?"

"I don't know. Should we see what Pete thinks? He's pretty close to her."

When they found Pete, they went to meet him. "The doctor is pretty busy. He's working alone today. The nurse sug-gested we set up a time to talk to him tomorrow morning," Pete said.

"I'll stay with her tonight. As long as Jamie has a place to stay," Essie offered.

"The nurse suggested that we all go home," Pete said. "They'll keep her heavily medicated for a couple of days. She promised to keep a close watch over her and let us know if there's any change."

"Lark and I were wondering if we should ask her about her son? Do you think she would want us to contact him?"

"No," he said abruptly. "I don't think we need to bother her. She has enough to worry about."

They agreed that Essie and Pete would meet with the doc-tor and let Lark know, then they would know where to go from there.

As Essie drove home, she realized how attached she'd be-come to Miss Ida. As she thought about the circumstances, she wondered what would happen to Jamie if she didn't get bet-ter? He was an innocent little boy that was brought into this world and abandoned by his parents. If not for this loving grandmother, he would have been cast into a system that no doubt would have destroyed his chance of ever becoming the happy, well-adjusted, seven-year-old boy he was now. Somehow, she had to find the words to explain to him that his grandmother might not make it.

CHAPTER SEVEN

At nine-thirty on Monday morning, Essie and Pete arrived at the hospital to see Dr. Morris. A nurse showed them to a small consultation room with three chairs and a small table. Dr. Morris, a small man, with a friendly attitude and an air of authority, entered and motioned for them to sit. His somber face told them the news wasn't good. They shook hands, and he sat.

"I'm sorry I don't have much time, so let us get to the matter at hand. I hear you want some information on Miss Ida Belle Sands," Dr. Morris said.

"Yes," Pete spoke up. "She's been staying with Essie since the last time she was in the hospital. She has no relatives around, so I guess you could say we're her caregivers."

"I've known Miss Ida for a long time," Dr. Morris said. "Does anyone know where her son is?"

"Not that we know. That's why we need to know if her condition is bad enough that we should start trying to find him," Pete said.

"I'm not going to get into the details of her illness. It's a complicated condition. The sad truth is, is that we've done what we can for her. Her body is too weak to fight back. Her time is limited, and all we can do for her is keep her as comfortable as possible."

Essie's voice cracked. "How long?"

"We have no way of knowing. It could be tomorrow or a week from now."

"Will she be able to communicate? She has her grandson

living with her. As far as we know, she has no arrangements made for him. He's only seven years old." Essie wiped a tear from her eye.

"Yes, I know Jamie. She'll be very aware of everything. There's nothing wrong with her mind. She'll be able to talk to her lawyer or whatever needs to be done. She needs to get her affairs in order. If she lets us know when she needs to be alert, we can cut back on her medication."

"Does she know how sick she really is?" Pete asked.

"I haven't talked to her yet. I wanted to talk to you first. I'm on my way as soon as I leave here."

"Do you want us there?" Essie asked.

"Knowing Miss Ida, I think it would be better if I do this alone. She'll want to pull herself together before she sees anyone. Just give her an hour or so."

Pete reached out to shake the doctor's hand. "Thank you, Dr. Morris. We appreciate you taking the time to talk to us."

He shook Pete's hand. "I'm sorry I didn't have better news for you. Miss Ida is a wonderful lady, and she's done a lot for this community."

Pete and Essie left, walking silently to the parking lot. As they got into Pete's vehicle, they looked at each other. Essie saw the same compassion in his eyes that she'd seen when she'd told him about her brother. She'd seen him with Miss Ida, and his affection for her was like that of a son. Could it be, for some unknown reason, that they didn't want it to be known that he was her son? He certainly had a father-like relationship with Jamie. The tear that trickled down his cheek revealed the pain he felt.

Essie sighed. "Can we go somewhere and get a cup of coffee? We need to discuss this before we see her. I don't know what to say to her."

The first thing Essie said as they were seated in the small cafe was, "What's going to happen to Jamie?"

Pete slumped in his chair, fiddling with the silverware in front of him. "I don't know, but we better act fast because, according to Dr. Morris, she doesn't have much time."

"We can't just turn Jamie over to the social workers. They could send him off to a place where we would never see him." Essie's voice squeaked as she tried to curb the panic that rose inside her.

Pete shook his head. "No way! I'll take him and make tracks before that happens." His fists tightened as he wadded the napkin into a small ball.

A feeling of horror ran through Essie. She could see Pete was rattled. "You mean kidnap him? Pete, you can't do that!"

"Yes, I could. I know my way around. I could take him places where we would never be found." He threw the napkin down and took a big swig from his cup.

"How do you think Miss Ida would react to me keeping Jamie?" She watched Pete intently.

Pete looked deep into her eyes. "Whoa! Do you know what you're saying? Do you realize the responsibility of raising a kid? You would be willing to do that?"

"I love that little rascal, and you would help me if there was something I couldn't handle, wouldn't you?"

"Of course, you know I would. But have you really thought about this?" He grabbed her hands.

"Some, but then one just imagines Miss Ida being around forever." She stared off into space. She couldn't comprehend her world without that witty, sassy little woman in it. In her wonderful way, she'd emerged as a live version of her nana.

"I wonder if she has arrangements made for him. She's organized. Maybe we should talk to her before we go making plans," Pete suggested.

"I don't think she has. It seems to be her biggest worry. What about Jamie's mom or dad? Do you think they have any say in this?" She watched for his reaction.

He shook his head. "I believe they gave up all legal rights to him."

"Do you think she would let me do this?" she blurted out. "I would even adopt him and make him my son." Even surprised at her own audacity, her excitement grew as the idea developed in her mind.

"I think she would be delighted to leave him in such capable and loving hands."

When they got back to the hospital, Miss Ida was alert and seemed to be waiting for them. Pete enfolded her in his arms. Standing on the opposite side of the bed, Essie saw him reach up and wipe a tear from his cheek. She bent over and put her arms around them both, the three of them embracing there, fervently soaking up the love they had for each other.

When they finally let go, Miss Ida said, "That could really mess up an old lady's powder."

Essie took her hand in hers. All she could manage to say was, "I'm so sorry."

"Yeah, me, too, but not so much for me as for Jamie." She stuck her chin in the air. "God will just have to wait until I find a good home for him before he takes me away."

"Atta girl. That's one of the things I love about you most, never giving up," Pete said.

A big tear rolled down Miss Ida's cheek. Her frail little body slumped in defeat, sat wrapped in a blanket and propped against a pillow. Her voice trembled as she spoke. "Doesn't look like I have much choice this time."

"Miss Ida, if I'm worthy in your eyes, I would love to take Jamie and raise him." Essie held her breath.

Miss Ida's eyes popped open wide, and she raised her hands feebly toward heaven. "Thank you, God," she mumbled. "There's no one I would rather have him with than you. Are you sure you want to do this?"

"Yes, I'm sure. You know how much I love that little boy." Essie's heart beat frantically as the picture unfolded before her.

"And he loves you, too. You make dying so much easier. May God bless you." Miss Ida held out her hands. "Now, come give me a big hug."

As Essie embraced the older woman, she knew she was also embracing the biggest undertaking ever entrusted to her, the raising of a precious human being. She felt, at that moment, the feeling every new parent must feel when holding their baby for the first time.

"Pete, please get hold of Rod Sheffield for me and have him see me as soon as possible," Miss Ida instructed. "He's my lawyer, and I have lots of things I need to get done. Let him know how urgent this is. Tell him that even I don't have that much influence with God, so if he wants me to put in a good word for him, he better get himself over here, stat." She chuckled. "Gee, I've been around the staff so long I'm beginning to speak their language."

Pete nodded. "We'll stop by his office on the way home. I'll get him here today, if possible."

"Thanks! You two better go and let this tired old body rest because I want to be at my best when Rod gets here."

Essie encircled the frail little lady in her arms. "Thanks for your confidence in me. I promise I'll do my best for Jamie, and I'll always keep your memory alive for him." It hurt her deeply to think of Miss Ida as a memory.

Miss Ida chuckled. "Maybe some of those memories would be better forgotten. Did I ever tell you about the time I tricked Jamie into eating broccoli? He loved apple fritters. I mixed small bits of broccoli in with the apples. When he asked me about the green, I told him it was green apples." She raised her hands. "God forgive me, but he ate broccoli for two years without knowing it, until he caught me one day. I could never get him to eat a fritter after that."

Essie laughed. "I guess I won't try to feed him apple fritters. Is it okay if I bring him to see you after school today?"

"Yes, I have so much to say to him. I hope God will give me the time and the right words so it won't be too hard for him. Being able to tell him that he'll be with you will make it easier. Now, get." Miss Ida shooed them away with her hand. "And if I don't make it till he gets here . . ." She hesitated. "Just tell him I love him from here to Mars. It's our little thing." Her eyes had that faraway look in them.

After they stopped by and saw Rod, Essie and Pete went straight to the school to talk to Lark. He told them he had put the search for Miss Ida's son into action.

"No doubt he'll show up looking for an inheritance. Where has he been all this time? I can't imagine a child abandoning their mother." Essie spread her hands in disgust.

Pete shook his head. "I have my doubts that he'll ever be found."

When Lark dropped Jamie off after school, as always with Joey in tow, Essie gave the boys a snack, and Lark sent them to the clubhouse.

"Does Jamie know how sick his grandma is?" Lark asked.

"No. I'm taking him to see her in a while. It's her place to tell him what she wants him to hear. It'll be easier for him to hear it from her."

"You sound like a mother already," Lark said with a grin. "Do you mind if I go with you? I need to say goodbye to Miss Ida."

"Of course. We'll leave in about an hour if that's okay."

"Good, I'll drop Joey off at the neighbor's and be right back." Lark put his arm around Essie and pulled her close. "Do you know how much I admire you for what you're doing? It's no easy job being a single parent, but I'll be here for you if you ever need me. I do have a lot of experience, you know." He gave her a prolonged kiss on the cheek.

"Oh, Lark, how can we make this all go away? Not that I don't want to be Jamie's mother, but I can't imagine this town without Miss Ida. I can't imagine me without her. It'll be like a swarm of honeybees without its queen."

Essie tried to prepare Jamie by telling him that his grandma would be hooked up to some tubes and that they were there so the nurses could give her medicine without sticking her with a needle each time. Jamie walked quietly into the room, hesitated for a second, then went right to his grandma's outstretched arms. Essie could see the tears trickle down Miss Ida's cheeks as she held her grandson close.

Essie gave Miss Ida a hug as well. "I'll be right outside in the lounge. You take all the time you want and send for me when you're ready. Lark's with me, and he wants to see you for a minute if you feel like it."

Essie could see the stress on Miss Ida's face. This was undoubtedly the hardest challenge she'd ever faced in her seventy-eight years of life. It would be the hardest thing Jamie had faced in his short seven years, and it would be Essie's job to help him through it.

Essie closed the door softly and walked back to the lounge.

Lark was pacing the floor. "How did it go?" he asked.

"Jamie was okay. He went right to her, but I'm sure she isn't looking forward to what she has to do."

"Miss Ida will do what she has to," Lark said.

As they sat waiting, Essie reflected on her life and how much it had changed in the last few months. She'd left Tulsa a broken, confused person with no thoughts of anyone except herself. Now she had never felt more a part of a community. She'd regained most of the confidence in herself that had been destroyed by her relationship with Brad, and she would be taking on one of the greatest responsibilities a person could ever have—the rearing of a child. No doubt there would be numerous obstacles along the way, but her friends had offered to help. They were true friends she knew she could count on when she really needed them. She said a short prayer of thanks and vowed to start worshiping on Sundays with the rest of the town.

When the nurse came for them, Miss Ida was holding Jamie in her arms. Essie could see they'd both been crying.

"You take this boy and get him some ice cream," Miss Ida said. "I promised him a double dip cone, even if he doesn't eat a bite of dinner, but just this once." Miss Ida pushed Jamie away and motioned for him and Essie to leave the room. Her eyes followed Jamie intently as Essie led him out the door.

Lark waited at the door and on Essie's nod, entered Miss Ida's room. Essie couldn't help herself but peek in on the two.

Lark stood looking down at the shadow of the former vibrant, perky little lady before entering the room. Essie told herself to give the two some privacy but couldn't turn away from the sad scene before her.

"Don't you make me cry, young man," Miss Ida said to Lark, as she held out her arms. "There have been enough tears around here. Somebody better start building an ark."

"They'll never make another one like you," Lark said as he bent to hug her. Essie could see the pain in Lark, his body shaking as he embraced the older woman.

Miss Ida chuckled. "The world better hope not."

Lark released the frail little matriarch and took both her hands in his. "I won't keep you. I know you must be tired. I just wanted to say hello."

"Might as well make it goodbye, but first, I have one thing to say to you before you go. Don't let that wonderful lady get away from you."

Now Essie felt even worse for eavesdropping. Was Miss Ida talking about Diana? Essie turned to go but caught Miss Ida's eyes over Lark's shoulder. Miss Ida winked at Essie.

"Take these words from an old lady, Essie is perfect for you, and you would make a beautiful family of four."

Lark held her tighter. "I'll see what I can do about that. Now get some rest."

He turned to leave, and Essie slipped back out into the corridor, her heart aching for more than one reason.

Miss Ida slipped quietly away two days later with her friend, Florence, holding her hand.

Her funeral was one of the biggest events Rosepoint had ever experienced. True to Miss Ida's nature, she'd requested it to be a gala occasion. One had to chuckle as the first song the choir sang was *Ain't Gonna Need This House No More.* In her last blaze of glory, she was dressed in red, a color known to be her favorite. The small church couldn't hold all the people, so it was arranged with Matt Simons to have the dinner at the community hall.

How appropriate—the death of Miss Ida coinciding with the death of their community hall. Matt Simmons had just announced there was to be no more use of the hall, as he planned to start renovations in two weeks. Miss Ida's son was not located.

Things settled into a routine quickly. Rod Sheffield stopped by with papers for Essie to sign. Miss Ida had left all her financial assets to Jamie, with Essie in charge until he came of age. She left her property to the town of Rosepoint, with the specification that it was used for whatever the town board decided best. Her grandfather had been Rosepoint's first mayor, so she had many items of historical value that were also left to the town.

Pete and Lark helped transfer Jamie's things, and Essie settled him into his own room upstairs. She'd thought about putting him in her brother's old room, but her subconscious kept her from doing that. Her grandmother's memorial to her brother would remain undisturbed.

Jamie, with his own personality and his love of bright colors, deserved his own choices. They went downtown and picked out a multi-colored spread and curtains. Essie furnished the room with a small table, two matching green chairs she'd found in the basement, and his toy chest brought over from his grandmother's. Over in one corner, she hung a bright red fishnet and filled it with his collection of stuffed animals. Brightly colored scatter rugs with various *Disney* characters were placed around the large room. She thought it looked rather gaudy, but Jamie was delighted.

Essie felt worried about him. He'd been quiet and withdrawn during their shopping trip, so the smile on his face was worth it when he saw the finished project. He'd not talked about Miss Ida since the funeral. If only she knew how to help him.

While Jamie was in school, Essie decided to start cleaning out some of the many papers and items her grandmother had collected over the years. She chuckled to herself as she realized what a pack rat her grandmother had been. Every bill she'd paid, marked with the date and check number and put in a large manilla envelope by the year, was neatly arranged in one drawer. Another held several vintage purses, all stuffed with tissue paper, each in its own plastic bag. As Essie pulled the purses out, she noticed a lone envelope at the bottom of the drawer. Written on it in bold letters was the word *KEEP*.

She tore the envelope open and took out two sheets of paper. One was the bill of sale for the community hall, and the other was an official-looking document. As she read, her heart leaped with joy. It was a statement drawn up by a law firm in Milwaukee, declaring that the community hall could not be used for anything other than the purpose for which it was built. It was signed by her grandfather and Matt Simmons.

What a sneak. He'd assumed no one would know about this since her grandfather's death. How clever of her grandfather to have provided this protection for future generations. Essie looked at her watch—noon. She jumped up and called Lark on his cell phone.

"You've got to come over right now!" she yelled into the phone.

"What's wrong?" he hollered back.

She could hear the panic in Lark's voice. "No, no, there's nothing wrong. It's good news." She couldn't control the excitement in her voice. "It's the community hall. It's safe! My grandpa saved it. You've got to come over now. God rest his soul. My grandpa saved it for us."

Lark laughed across the line. "I'll be right over. You better calm down. I don't want you to have a heart attack. You almost gave me one."

She hung up and ran to the door to wait for him. When Lark got out of his truck, she stood on the porch waving the document at him. "Read this!" She poked the paper at him.

He took it from her and read.

"It's legal, isn't it?" she asked. "It's by a lawyer. It has to be legal." She watched his face as he examined the paper, and when he broke into a big grin, he grabbed her and swung her around in circles.

"It's legal, all right. We've got him now. He can't take our hall away from us. Where did you find this?"

"I was cleaning out some of Nana's things, and I found it in a drawer. Thank God she never threw anything away. We had better do something with this quick. He's starting to remodel soon." She walked in circles, pumping her arms in the air.

"Not now, he isn't. I'll take this. I know exactly what to do with it." He picked her up and swung her around again.

That afternoon as she prepared dinner, she discovered she needed several things from the store. One thing she'd promised herself was to never take shortcuts in preparing healthy meals for Jamie. It was a nice day, so she decided to walk instead of driving.

She bundled up and headed down the sidewalk, enjoying the brisk, cool air as it hit her in the face. The houses on this end of town were all older. It was the original part of town, Essie guessed. She passed Mr. Johnson's hardware store and the small apartment above it where Pete lived. Across the street was a newer building occupied by the bank and Rosepoint's very small library. The grocery store stood on the corner next to the library. Sam Howard, the owner, whom she'd met at Miss Ida's funeral, greeted her.

"Good afternoon to you, Essie. I see you're enjoying one of our beautiful Wisconsin fall days."

"Indeed, I am. I'm just learning to put on an extra layer of clothes."

"You haven't seen anything yet. Just wait until it gets thirty below."

She pulled her coat closer to her body. "I'm not looking forward to that."

"I know, that's when we would all like to skip out to Florida or someplace warmer. Speaking of skipping out, is there any word from Miss Ida's son?"

"Not that I know of. I feel bad that we couldn't locate him." She did feel bad, especially for Miss Ida. She couldn't imagine what her last days had been like, not knowing where her child was. But she'd never mentioned him to anyone of them.

"It happens more often than we know. Take that Sawyer

boy, for instance. Went off to Chicago and became a big-time lawyer. It went to his head, and he started neglecting his family." He walked behind the counter and started checking her groceries. "I was pretty good friends with his brother and still keep in touch with him. From what he tells me, all his oldest boy wanted from his dad was a little attention, and all his dad kept telling him was, I'm doing this for you. When his mom died, the boy took off and hasn't been heard from since. Now that the dad retired, he realized what a terrible mistake he made."

"It's sad that sometimes we don't realize our mistakes until it's too late," Essie said.

"Yes, I wonder if some of that stuff going on over at the old Sawyer place might have something to do with that boy. I hear he spent some fun summers there with his grandparents when he was a young kid. Makes sense that he would come back here where he has happy memories."

News spread fast about the community hall. Lark, the mayor, and Rod Shefield went to see Matt Simmons. Matt claimed he'd forgotten about the agreement. They left him an angry man, threatening to close the building and let it sit until it rotted.

When Lark told Essie, she asked, "Do you really think he'll shut it down to community use? Maybe when he thinks about it for a while, he'll change his mind. We know how he likes his money."

Lark shook his head. "He can also be stubborn. I've been thinking . . . we need to call a board meeting anyway to discuss what's to be done with Miss Ida's property. We can take care of both matters at one time."

Thinking of Miss Ida's large Victorian house and what an asset it would be for Rosepoint, Essie felt a warm feeling run through her veins. "It'll be a fine museum with so much of her grandfather's memorabilia to fill its rooms. One thing I know, it's a grand old house, and nothing should be done to change it." Watching the expression on Lark's face, she thought she could detect a hint of disappointment.

Clearing his throat, Lark ducked his head and quietly said, "I have a few ideas."

Lark did indeed have a few ideas. They'd been churning in his head for a couple of years, and now, the perfect solution presenting itself, he'd been preparing his speech to the board. He knew the need couldn't be denied, and it hadn't occurred to him that almost everyone wouldn't go along with it. Ever since he'd been in Rosepoint and involved with the children, he noticed the lack of activities for them after school and on weekends. His dream of establishing a sort of rec center for them where they could congregate safely with some sort of monitoring grabbed onto this solution and wouldn't let go.

Its location, in the center of town and not far from the school, seemed perfect. That was why he'd been so surprised when Essie mentioned changes were taboo. There was no way it could be used as it stood. Walls would have to be moved, bathrooms be altered, and the kitchen commercialized. He knew how much Essie loved children. There was a slight tug at his conscience at the thought of any kind of controversy with her, but hopefully, when she heard his ideas, she'd come around to his side because this plan had been developing so long that he just couldn't let it go.

When Lark stopped on Sunday morning to pick Jamie up for church, Essie, dressed and ready to go, greeted them. "I think it's about time I show thanks to God for all of the blessings he's been giving me."

"We'll all be glad to welcome you to our congregation. Just a little warning though, before the day is over, there's a great possibility that you'll be recruited to sing in the choir, teach Sunday school, and probably work in the nursery."

Essie laughed. "I'll take my car and meet you there."

Indeed, Essie was asked to join many of the different activities within the church. She received warm welcomes from those whom she knew and was introduced to those she'd not met. True to the nature of Rosepoint, she found herself drawn further into the midst of the friendly little community.

As Essie waited for Jamie to come from Sunday school, many of the townspeople stopped to welcome her. Her heart fell when she saw him walking alone and dejected. She grabbed their coats from the rack and looked around for Lark. He was deep in conversation with the pastor. Deciding not to wait for him, she helped Jamie on with his coat, and they slipped out the door.

"Tell me what you did in Sunday school today," she said as she unlocked the door to the house.

"We made these pictures." Jamie handed her the paper he had clutched in his hand. "It's s'posed to be our family."

Her heart melted as she took the folded paper and opened it to see two crudely sketched figures. Jamie had drawn himself, standing alone. At a distance was a lone girl figure.

"Tell me about it." His head dropped, and she could see his reluctance to talk. She put her arm around him. "It's okay, sweetheart, it's a nice picture." She knelt and looked him in the eye. "I'm guessing this is me," she said, pointing to the taller figure with longer hair.

Jamie nodded his head shyly.

She took the picture and folded it to where they stood, touching each other. She showed it to him. "Do you know how proud I am to be your family?" She pulled him into her arms.

"Miss Essie, how come I don't have a mama and daddy like everybody else?"

Her heart melted at how sad he sounded. What could she say to him that would make him realize how special he was? She was surprised at the words that seemed to flow from her mouth.

"God sometimes needs helpers and makes special boys and girls for that purpose. He knew your grandma would be all alone, so I think he made you to be with her. Then, he knew I needed someone to love. So he sent you to me." She watched his reaction closely.

"You can be my make-believe mama," Jamie said somberly.

She tickled him. "I don't want to be no make-believe mama. I want to be a real, genuine, honest-to-goodness mama who loves her little red-headed boy a whole bunch." She tickled him again and had him laughing and rolling on the floor to get away from her. "Now, you go change your clothes so we can have some good old sloppy barbecues for lunch."

He got up and ran up the stairs. "Okay, Mama."

Essie stopped short as her jaw flew open. The word mama came so naturally from his mouth. She couldn't imagine a greater pleasure. She marveled at the fate that brought her to Rosepoint and at the gifts that were hers to enjoy.

CHAPTER EIGHT

The following Monday, the painters were scheduled to start their job, depending on the weather, which was unpredictable at that time of the year.

"Have you decided on your colors?" Pete asked as he finished tightening the hinges on the cabinet doors.

"It can't be anything but white," Essie said. "I want everything painted in the original colors."

"What about the trim? Want to brighten it up a little?" he asked.

"No, I'm keeping it white also. That was the original color."

"What! No purple? Or maybe hot pink?" he teased.

Although Essie knew he was teasing, her mouth flew open in horror as she imagined her nana's house with purple trim. "Nana would turn in her grave if I painted her beloved house purple or pink."

"What about the wallpaper? Have you got that all picked out?"

"I have a sample book here. It's so hard to decide."

He took the book and flipped the pages. "Let me help. Eenie, meenie, miney, moe." He pointed to a brightly colored sample with huge diamond shapes placed in crooked rows across the page.

"Wipe that grin off your face. You're not helping me pick out anything. I would have a rainbow house if I took your advice." She grabbed the book and set it aside.

"I saw a rainbow house once, honestly. It was in . . ." A startled look crossed Pete's face.

"Are you kidding? Where was it?" Could she get him to mention a location?

"I can't remember. You better decide on the paper soon. It'll have to be ordered."

"The paper hangers won't be here until next week. I was told the store could get it in two days. I'm not looking forward to all the chaos around here."

"Get used to it," Pete said. "You have a kid now, whose middle name is Chaos."

"He called me mama," Essie blurted out. She ran to Pete, grabbed him around the neck, and squeezed him.

"Wow!" Pete gleamed. "In my opinion, that makes you officially a mama."

"I'm so afraid, Pete. What if I can't do this?"

"Of course you can do it. Where's all that courage you showed when you made your promise to Miss Ida? You'll learn as you go." He grabbed her by the arms. "If you make mistakes, pick yourself up and go on. It's human nature to err."

"But I want to be a perfect mama."

"Jamie doesn't need a perfect mama. What he needs is a loving, responsible person who's there for him when he needs them. I believe that person is you, and so did Miss Ida."

"I hope you're right. Thank you for believing in me." Essie gave him a hug.

"I'm right." Pete held her at arm's length. "What are you and Jamie doing this weekend?"

"I'm taking him and Joey ice skating. I hear there's a rink over in Mt. Harmon. Woe is me, though. I haven't been on ice since high school."

"I wish I could go with you, but I promised to help Mr. Johnson at the store. His nephew is getting married. Is Lark going?"

"No, he's busy."

Pete chuckled. "All you have to do is remember what I told you. When you fall, pick yourself up and go on. You may have to stop and rub your bruises now and then."

"I'm actually looking forward to it." Essie stuck her chin in the air. "I used to be a pretty good skater."

"You guys have a good time. I have to go now." Pete waved as he got into his truck.

"Jamie, are you ready to go? Joey will be here shortly," Essie hollered up the stairs.

"I can't find my skates, Miss Es . . ." Jamie stopped short.

Essie's heart skipped a beat. She longed to hear him call her Mama again. Running up the stairs, she saw him sitting on the bed, a tear trickling down his cheek. She put her arm around him. "What's wrong, sweetheart?"

"I forgot. I'm s'pose to call you Mama."

She squeezed him to her. "I would like for you to call me Mama, but if you forget, that's okay. Just remember, no matter what you call me, I'm always going to be here for you, and I will always be your mama. Now, let's find your skates."

When Lark dropped Joey off, he ran upstairs to join Jamie.

"I think he might want these." Lark shook his head as he held out Jamie's skates. "I'm sorry, I have to run. Thank you for taking Joey. He's so excited."

"No problem. I just hope we all come back in one piece. It's been a while since I've skated," Essie said.

"A few bumps and bruises won't hurt anyone. I always carry a box of *Band-Aids* with me." He chuckled. "Oh. I'll tell you before I forget, there's an open meeting tomorrow evening to talk about the community hall and to discuss Miss Ida's house, if you are interested."

"You bet I'm interested. I'll be there with bells on," she answered.

Activity at the rink was low due to a local football game. Essie helped the boys with their skates and tightened the laces on her own. She slowly guided them onto the ice, holding each by the hand. She was surprised by the skill the two seven-year-old boys had. She remembered her first time on the ice as a ten-year-old and her trouble standing. As long as she held onto the boys, they glided slowly along.

"How would you like to do a turn?" Essie asked. "I'll help you. Come, Joey, I'll show you. Jamie, you stand there and don't move." She took Joey by the hand and slowly guided his body into a turn.

"Look, Mama, look." She turned to see Jamie trying to mimic the turn on his own.

"No, Jamie! Be careful," she called out, reaching for him just as he fell. She knelt beside him. "Are you okay? I'm sorry, Jamie, this is all my fault."

"Ow." Jamie grabbed his arm. She could see the tears in his eyes. Gathering him up, being careful to avoid the injured arm, she helped him to his feet.

"We have to get you to the doctor. Come on, Joey, we need to hurry." She led them to the bench, took her scarf and made a sling for Jamie's arm, and helped them get their skates off. She noticed his arm was beginning to swell.

As she tried hard to calm the sick feeling inside her, the guilt overwhelmed her. Why had she left him alone? He was just a little boy who depended on her to protect him, and she'd failed. Her old doubts returned. Was she really capable of the task set before her? What did she know about being a parent?

When they got back to Rosepoint, she drove straight to the hospital. Dr. Morris immediately took them into his office. "Jamie, tell me what happened to your arm."

"I was ice skating, and I fell. It hurts awful." Jamie sniffled.

"Let me see." Dr. Morris gently took Jamie's arm out of the

sling and examined it carefully. Using his thumb, he pushed on different spots around the elbow, Jamie jumping when he touched a sensitive spot. Patting him on the back, Dr. Morris looked at him and smiled. "You're a lucky young man," he said. "You have no broken bones, just bruised up quite badly." He walked to a cabinet and came back with an arm sling and a jar of cream. Handing the cream to Essie, he tied the sling around Jamie's neck and placed his arm inside. "Just rub that cream on, and it will help with the soreness," he said to Essie.

"How long should he wear this?" Essie put her arm around Jamie's shoulder.

"He'll know when it needs to come off. Won't you, Jamie?" Dr. Morris asked

Jamie nodded his head shyly.

"Are you guys hungry?" Essie asked when they left the hospital. "How about we stop by and pick up a pizza? It'll be your reward for being so good."

"Yeah!" they both yelled, getting into the back seat and Joey helping Jamie buckle his seatbelt.

Lark came to pick Joey up at six o'clock. "Whoa!" he said when he saw Jamie. "What happened to you?"

"He fell while I was turning," Joey said. "But it's not broke or nothing. And he's gotta wear that sling till he knows when to take it off. Then we came back here and had pizza. It was our 'ward 'cause we was so good." Joey looked pleased with his diagnostic explanation.

Lark grinned. "You better take a deep breath after all that." He looked at Essie.

"What more can I say?" Essie shrugged.

"You thank Miss Essie and get your skates," Lark told Joey. "Wait in the truck, and I'll be right there."

"Thank you, Miss Essie." Joey ran to get his skates, and

Jamie followed him.

Lark draped his hand over Essie's shoulder. "Thank you for taking Joey. I don't do enough things with him. It's hard to make the time."

"You're thanking me when I almost let my son break his arm? I feel awful. How can you trust me with Joey? I'm a terrible mother!" She turned her head upward. "I'm sorry, Miss Ida," she said, her eyes starting to burn.

He grabbed her by both arms. "Look here, beautiful lady, you're a wonderful mother. Accidents happen, especially on the ice, so don't go putting yourself down. I trust you with Joey as much as I trust myself." He gave her a kiss on the cheek. "I have to go now. Joey's waiting." He squeezed her tight, then let her go.

Essie felt good and bad all at the same time. Good that Lark trusted her with Joey, and bad that she'd let Jamie get hurt. She knew accidents happened, but she was trying so hard. Would it ever get easier?

Anticipating a large crowd, the board meeting had been scheduled at the school where rows of seats were lined up across the auditorium floor. Essie, running a little late waiting for the babysitter, eased into a chair toward the back just as the meeting was about to start.

The mayor stood to speak.

"As most of you know, we've called this special meeting to discuss two important matters. The first concerns the community hall. A committee of three went to see Mr. Simmons, and although he admitted to signing that paper, he believes it's his right to ignore it because the other party is no longer living. I'm afraid Mr. Simmons is very angry with us. He's threatened to lock the hall up and let it sit there and rot, so it's our opinion that we let this matter rest for a while, and maybe he'll come to realize he'll be better off leaving things the way they are. Are there other opinions on this?"

One man toward the middle of the room hollered out, "I think you're right. Let Matt pout a while. He'll start missing that rent money, and he'll come slinking back."

"Then is everyone in agreement with letting this matter rest for a bit?" the mayor asked.

Amid a few stifled laughs, shouts of agreement rang out across the audience.

"Okay, it's agreed. Now, as I'm sure most of you have heard, Miss Ida, whom we miss terribly, so generously left her property to the city. So our next order of business is to decide the best way to use it. You've all had time to think about this. The floor is open to ideas."

Two hands went up immediately, and Essie could see one of them was Lark's. She looked forward to hearing his ideas, but the mayor pointed to a middle-aged lady whom Essie knew worked for the mayor.

"Yes, Martha, you have the floor. Don't worry, you'll all get your turn, but I work with this lady, and if I don't treat her right, I might not get any more of those delicious brownies she makes."

Among laughter, Martha came forward and took the microphone. "For many years, I, along with many of you, have admired Miss Ida's house. As always one of the landmarks I showed visitors from out of town, I feel it radiates this town's respect for the preservation of our past. Isn't this what we're most proud of when we drive down our streets lined with these beautiful old homes? Therefore, I would like to see it opened to the public, perhaps staged with an attendant dressed appropriately for that period to give tours. We could even charge a small fee."

In the back, Essie listened with interest. What Martha said made sense. Before she realized it, Essie was on her feet seeking permission to speak. "I think that's a perfect use of the building. In my opinion, it's very important to not destroy the rich history of one of this town's greatest treasures. In fact, we could turn it into a museum. If I understand it, there are many items of historical value saved by Miss Ida's grandfather, who was the first mayor of Rosepoint." Looking around, Essie tried to decipher the thoughts of the townspeople. "This idea certainly gets my vote." Suddenly embarrassed, she quickly sat down.

The mayor rose to his feet. "Are there any more comments on Martha's suggestion?" When no one spoke, Essie was disappointed. "Then we'll move on. Lark, I think you have something to say."

Lark stepped forward and took the microphone. "Although Martha's idea would probably be workable, I feel there's a far greater need and a more realistic used to be made of this unexpected opportunity. It has been my privilege to work with the young people here for the last six years. I've seen firsthand the lack of supervised activities, especially after school and on weekends. I know the house would need some work, but isn't it worth it to invest in the lives of our youth. After all, they are our future."

"What kind of work are you talking about?" one lady asked.

He cleared his throat and fiddled nervously with the mike. "It needs to be opened up into bigger rooms, and the bathroom and kitchen modified."

Essie was seething. She thought she could see Lark looking straight at her.

"Where are we going to get the money for that?" someone else asked.

"That's something we'll have to work on. We can do fundraisers and a lot of hands-on volunteer labor. It won't be easy, but it will be worth it. Anyone who's a good parent and cares about the needs of their child will understand this."

Why hadn't he discussed this with her before? Well, she wasn't going to stand by and let him destroy Miss Ida's house. He'd see. She thought of standing up and telling him just what she thought, but instead, she grabbed her jacket and slipped quietly out the door.

Lark watched as Essie left. His heart pounded loudly as he tried to recall what he'd said that might have upset her. His purpose, so intent on convincing all of Rosepoint of turning Miss Ida's house into a rec center for the youth, was the right thing to do. Not easy to let go of in his own mind, it was something worth fighting for. Surely, the great service his idea would bring to the youth of this town could override the determination to save Miss Ida's house. After all, it's not like the house would be torn down, just a few changes on the inside. He'd talk to Essie and explain it to her. She'd come around. After all, he knew her to be a reasonable person, and most of all, she was a parent first.

Lark suddenly caught a sharp breath. The thought still lingering in his mind, he knew right away what he'd said. He'd said, *any good parent who cared about the needs of their child would understand that need.* What a fool he'd been. He excused himself and went after her, just to see her drive away as he came out the door.

A sick feeling rose up in Essie's stomach as she hurried to her car, wiping the tears from her eyes as she slid inside and closed her door behind her. Still trying to convince herself what she heard Lark say was a mistake, she took a deep breath, laid her head on the steering wheel, and tried to calm herself. As she lifted her head and started the engine, she glanced out the side window and saw Lark coming out the door, no doubt looking for her. She slid the gear into *Drive* and drove off.

After sending the sitter home, she made a cup of tea, turned off all the lights, and plopped down on the sofa. She had no intention of answering the door or the phone tonight. She would show Lark Winters what a good parent she could be, and if he wanted to go messing with Miss Ida's house, he'd have a fight on his hands. The more she thought about it, the more determined she became to start a campaign to save Miss Ida's house.

What Lark said the previous evening hung over Essie like a rain cloud, ready to open and pour its contents down on her. She could think of nothing else, and her emotions went from sadness to anger to determination. Knowing in all fairness that Lark had every right to fight for what he believed in, she didn't see how he could choose to alter a grand old house, especially Miss Ida's, and destroy its history without a sliver of guilt. The thing that hurt her most was the indication that she didn't care about the needs of the youth. It seemed especially odd that he'd never talked to her about his idea.

Essie jotted down several points she wanted to make, and that afternoon when Lark dropped Jamie off, she was ready for him. She watched as he parked his truck and climbed down from the cab. As the boys ran on ahead of him, it seemed to Essie his steps faltered as he saw her waiting.

"Hi." He jingled the coins nervously in his pocket and sat beside her on the steps.

"Hi." Then she'd purposely not said anything else. She waited for him to continue the conversation.

He reached for her hand. Looking her straight in the eyes, he said, "Essie, I'm sorry if I said anything that hurt you. You must know that the last thing I want to do is upset you. I realize now I should have discussed my idea with you and not sprung it on you like that in front of the whole town. Certainly because you have other ideas for the use of Miss Ida's house doesn't mean you're any less of a concerned parent. My words didn't exactly come out as I meant them to."

She pulled her hand from his grip and looked at him seriously. "You have the right to fight for what you want, but you must know, so do I."

"You do have that right, but it's just when this opportunity came along, it seemed the perfect solution. Rosepoint will likely never be able to build a rec center, so it will probably never have one. You know how important kids are to me."

She looked at him sternly. "And they aren't to me? I'm a parent, too, you know."

He stood and looked down at her. "You're taking my words the wrong way again. I know what a good parent you are, and I know how you love kids. Essie, I care for you. I don't want this thing to come between us."

Essie could see the pleading in his eyes. "I'm not against a rec center," she said. "It's just the wrong use for Miss Ida's house."

Beyond the shadow overhanging her, life went on for Essie. She picked out wallpaper, paint, light fixtures, doorknobs, hinges, and various other things Pete suggested for the house. The contractors finished their job, cleaned up after themselves, and left everything neat and orderly.

Her satisfaction turned to elation as her mind encompassed every detail. The bedrooms with their antebellum style wallpaper, and large wooden rods newly hung with rich burgundy, deep green, and royal blue drapes, each chosen thoughtfully to coordinate with the Persian style rugs she'd found at an antique store in Mt. Harmon. The faded gold rope that adorned the four-poster bed in her bedroom had been replaced, and Nana's handmade quilts were spread lovingly on each bed. Over by the window, Nana's old sewing machine stood as another reminder of the precious memories Essie held in her heart. Sadness encompassed her as she thought of Miss Ida's house and all the precious history destined to be destroyed unless she could put a stop to it.

Jamie's room had been painted bright blue at his request, which made it even gaudier in Essie's eyes. She didn't care if it made him happy. Only her brother's room underwent no changes.

Basking in her surroundings, the shrill ringing of the phone brought her out of her reverie. "Good morning," she cheerfully said until she recognized the voice on the other end of the line. "Brad, what do you want?" she asked abruptly.

"Is that any way to greet an old boyfriend?"

"I have nothing to say to you. Why are you calling?" She thought about just hanging up, but her curiosity wouldn't let her.

"That's funny because I have a lot to say to you. Like how you embarrassed me by taking off and leaving me alone to face my parents when they showed up for dinner. A dinner you invited them to, I might add."

"Your parents showed up every Sunday. I'm sure they got over it."

"I see you have the same old attitude, doing everything to mess up my life," Brad said, snarling over the line.

"Then I guess you don't have to worry about that anymore. If it boosts your pride, just tell everyone you kicked me out." She waited for his reply, then, understanding his hesitation, said, "You already have, haven't you?"

"Whose life are you worming yourself into now? I bet you have some pretty boy on the line?" he asked sarcastically.

"Goodbye, Brad." She hung up. That old feeling of inadequacy came forcing itself back in as she sat in the nearest chair and covered her face with her hands. Was she really worming her way into Lark's life, as Brad had said? Had she *messed up* his relationship with Diana? She thought of the kiss she saw between the two of them at the restaurant. It suddenly became clear what had to be done. Her life had new meaning since Jamie came to live with her, and even though Lark apologized, his comment about a parent caring about their child's needs still weighed heavy on her mind. Her responsibility to Jamie took precedence over all else.

Still bothered by the unexpected call from Brad, Essie awoke with a startle. For an instant, she lapsed back into the dream that had awakened her.

She found herself in a strange place, surrounded by people with large hands pushing her forward into a lake with churning waters. On the far side, she could see Jamie struggling to stay afloat. Between them sat Lark, drifting safely in a boat, beckoning to her. The longing within her screamed for attention, yet she pressed forward toward Jamie with a strength she didn't know she had. As she reached him and enfolded him safely in her arms, she turned to see Lark's boat drifting away, his hand stretched out to her, with a look of helplessness on his face.

Shaken by the dream, she recalled an article she'd once read that every dream had a meaning. It would have been so easy for her to get in that boat and for the two of them to rescue Jamie. Had her determination to do this on her own pushed Lark too far? The look on his face as he drifted away haunted her. Yet, in real life, when she'd said no to him, within hours, Diana was back in the picture. Or had she ever been gone? She felt more confused than ever.

She woke Jamie and got him ready for school. When they arrived, she gave him an extra big hug. "Bye, sweetie. You have a good day."

Jamie jumped out of the car. "Bye, Mama." It still amazed her every time he called her that. It came so easy for him to say, yet it was a title she'd yet to prove worthy of. Try as she may, she couldn't wipe the smile off her face.

Dark and dreary clouds spread their gloom all morning, but at four o'clock, the season's first snowflakes began to fall. Jamie's face flushed with excitement. He rushed outside, spread his arms, and ran around in circles.

Fascinated by what she saw, Essie watched Jamie as he stuck out his tongue and let the cool snowflakes melt in his mouth. She put on her coat and went to join him.

It snowed steadily all through the night. The heavy snow clung to the branches of the lone tree in the front yard, gently bending them downward. The few small cones that still clung to the tree peeked out among its branches, desperately trying to hang on like a baby clung to its mother. It reminded Essie of a scene on a Christmas card. Fresh bunny tracks ran through the yard as if the little animal had been frolicking in the snow. A few stray leaves that had escaped burial blew across the top of the freshly fallen snow.

Essie pulled herself away from the scene, made a pot of coffee, and went to wake Jamie. He rolled over and stretched.

"Time to get up, sleepyhead." She sat beside him and gently caressed his back.

Suddenly Jamie curled into the fetal position. "Oh, my belly. I don't think I should go to school today. I'm awful sick. What if I give everybody my belly ache?" He looked at Essie and groaned again.

Struggling to keep a straight face, she turned her head to the side. "Maybe you're right. I have some medicine that will make it go away, but it tastes pretty bad. And I'm really disappointed because now who's going to help me make a snowman after school?"

Jamie sat straight up in bed and giggled. "It was a joke. I'm not really sick." He stood up and pounded his stomach.

Essie whistled a sigh of relief. "You pulled that one over on me. I thought sure I would have to take you to see Dr. Morris."

"Did I really fool you, Mama?" Jamie's eyes glowed with mischief.

"You sure did. I was thinking I would have to make that snowman all by myself." She pulled the covers down and encircled him in a big hug.

After dropping Jamie at school, she headed straight home. Chuckling to herself, she thought of his attempt at the oldest trick in the book. Somehow that made motherhood seem more real. Gloating in her own ego, Essie couldn't imagine her life without her little boy.

The chiming of the doorbell interrupted her as she sat down to eat her lunch. There he stood, dressed from head to toe in snow pants, coat, gloves, and a bright orange cap pulled down over his ears. It had been a few days since she'd seen Pete.

Laughing at him bundled up like a fat snowman, she said, "You look like you're ready to battle the elements."

"I am, with weapon in hand." He held up a bright yellow snow shovel.

"Come on in. I'll fix you a tuna sandwich," she offered.

"Nope! I've already eaten. I'm going to shovel your walk before I take off all this garb."

"Of course, the good Samaritan at work. I was going to tackle it after lunch," Essie said.

"With what?" Pete asked. "I bet your grandmother didn't own a snow shovel. I'm sure she had a service that did it for her."

"Everybody has a shovel of some kind. It might not be a pretty yellow one like yours, but so what?" she retorted.

Pete shook his head from side to side with a smirk on his face. "Go eat your lunch."

Half an hour later, he was finished shoveling and back at her door. "So tell me," Pete said as he took the last of his snowsuit off. "What's been going on in your life lately? Still like being a mother?"

Essie couldn't help the smile that crossed her face. "I love being a mother. Jamie finally got rid of that sling. All the kids thought it was cool, so he sort of played it up. This morning he tried the old sick routine on me. He was so cute."

"How about yourself? What are you doing for Essie?" he asked with concern.

"I have Jamie to do for. He's the most important thing in my life. I don't need anything else," she stated firmly.

"What about Lark? Are you still seeing him?"

"If you mean dating? No, I'm not." Essie lowered her head and turned away from him.

"Okay, I know that look. Tell me what's going on."

She shrugged her shoulders. "He and Diana are together."

"Oh, that again. Are you sure?" Pete asked.

"I'm sure. He asked me to go out with him, and when I told him no, he was with her that same day."

"Whoa! Whoa! You said no! Essie, what's going on here? Are you playing games with Lark?"

She looked Pete sternly in the eyes. "I don't play games with people. I just told him I needed to spend this time with Jamie. Besides, he's busy recruiting people for his project for a rec center. I'm sure he's gotten his claws into you, hasn't he?"

Pete looked at her, shook his head, and picked up her coat from the chair. "Come on, you need to get away from here. We're going for a ride."

"Where are we going?" she asked, not moving from her spot.

"I want to show you something. Have you ever seen the Amish country?"

"No, I don't believe I have. What's the Amish country?"

Pete explained. "It's where people live simply and peace-fully, with no modern conveniences complicating their lives."

"I didn't know there were any of those places left anymore. You're still talking about the United States of America, aren't you?"

"Mere miles from here. Come on." He summoned her with his hand.

Essie stepped forward as he held out her coat for her.

As they got further out of town, Essie noticed the landscape changing into more natural scenery. Here there were no power lines connecting to the big boxy homes, no fancy cars in the driveway, only huge barns and acres and acres of open fields. Occasionally, they met a lone buggy, pulled by a big workhorse, and carrying an Amish family. It had a soothing effect on her. The smell of the cool, unpolluted air hung loosely around her, and she could feel the tension draining from her body as she began to relax.

Without a word, Pete pulled to the side of the road and turned the engine off. He got out and motioned for her to follow. Leaning against the truck, he spread his hand toward the open view. The captivating scene opened up before them, unfolding into a panoramic view of endlessness, exposing a vast white expanse of snow-covered trees and rolling hills.

In the middle of the barren field stood an old piece of abandoned farm machinery, almost majestic in stature, embracing the elements with dignity. The beauty of it overwhelmed her. She stood speechless, breathing the fresh, crisp air into her lungs.

Finally, Pete spoke. "You see, life doesn't have to be complicated."

She sighed heavily. "It's so peaceful here."

"I'm sorry, Essie." He spoke to her with concern in his

voice.

"About what?" She was puzzled by his sudden change of subject.

"I know you have feelings for Lark. I'm sorry you think you don't have room for him in your life. But are you sure about this?"

She hesitated a moment, all the reasons rushing through her mind. "I need this time with Jamie. I have so much to learn."

"Millions of women and children have men in their lives. It's called a family. They learn together."

"Are you forgetting about Diana?" Essie slumped against the car.

"Have you ever talked to him about her? Does he know how you feel? Fight for your man, Essie," Pete said.

"He always runs back to her," she said, determined to make Pete understand how she felt.

"Then stop pushing him away from you," he spoke sternly.

Was she really pushing Lark away? she wondered. Troublesome thoughts flooded her mind. If he cared so much for her, why was Diana always there? Ever present in her mind was that kiss she'd seen with her own eyes. Pete couldn't possibly understand. She remembered Diana in Lark's kitchen and how familiar she was with her surroundings. How often was she there, and how many times had she cooked for Lark and Joey? And there was Miss Ida's house. Yes, she was doing the right thing. She and Jamie would be just fine on their own. Besides, she had her own project. She would do all she could to preserve Miss Ida's house. That certainly wouldn't make it easy for her and Lark to be together. It seemed like maybe they were destined to be on opposite sides.

Refreshed by the peaceful ride in the country, Essie felt a renewed vitality about herself as Pete dropped her off at home.

She busied herself planning one of Jamie's favorite dishes for supper and was baking cookies when he came home from school, a little disappointed, yet somehow a little happy as she watched Lark drive away without stopping in to say hello.

It was eleven thirty when Essie got out of the beauty shop the next day. She went home, tossed a salad for lunch, surfed through the channels, and turned off the TV. Restless and bored, she decided to go for a walk. After bundling up in her winter garb, she stepped out into the bright sunshine that was already melting the first snowfall of the season. It reminded her of a promise to help Jamie build a snowman. There would be plenty more opportunities she knew, but that excitement of the first snow had passed, and she felt like she'd failed him. She felt even worse as she passed a sagging snowman, its scarf untied and its carrot nose tilting lazily toward the ground.

As she walked carefully on the slippery sidewalk, she realized she was nearing the old Sawyer farm. When she noticed tire tracks in the snow leading to the backyard, her gaze followed around the corner of the house where she could see the tail end of what looked like a black *4Runner*. Immediately she recognized the small decal of a badger placed in the upper right-hand corner of the back window. There was no doubt it was Pete's vehicle. Determined to find out what he was doing there, she marched down the tire tracks toward his truck. As she passed the broken window, she heard voices coming from inside.

"Then it's a deal," Pete was saying.

"You'll have the money Friday. I'll contact you, and we can meet wherever you want."

"Excellent," Pete said. "Now, let's get out of here before anyone sees us."

Panic overtook Essie as she turned and retraced her steps.

She walked as fast as she could until she got to the corner. Looking back, she saw no sign of Pete's vehicle. She gave a sigh of relief as she slipped around the corner and out of sight.

Her heart pounded as she walked back home. What was Pete up to? Was there a dark side to this wonderful, mysterious man who had become her best friend? Her thoughts went to the conversation she'd heard in the grocery store. What kind of deal was he talking about? And why was he so afraid of being seen? She wondered what would have happened if he'd caught her lurking outside that broken window.

CHAPTER NINE

That evening when Jamie got home from school, he chattered excitedly about the Halloween party they would have at school. "We have to dress up funny. Me and Jamie want the best costumes there, so everybody can laugh at us."

"Oh, you do, huh? What do you think will make everybody laugh?"

"We don't know yet. Will you help us, Mama?"

"Of course I will. We'll fix you up so funny all the kids will be rolling on the floor laughing at you." Essie thought back through all the years of her mom transforming her into angels, monsters, and characters from the movies and popular fairy tales.

"Jimmy is gonna be Frankenstein, and Timmy is gonna be Dracula. So we can't be them." Jamie tipped his head to one side, stuck his finger to the corner of his mouth, and stood contemplating his dilemma.

"Anybody can be scary like that," Essie said. "Maybe something with red on top so we can use your hair as part of your costume. How about a carrot? Your hair is the right color."

"Yeah, that's funny. My grandma used to call me *carrot top* when she was teasing me. What can Joey be?" Jamie asked.

"Let's think about it. What color is his hair?"

He squinted his eyes together. "He sort of has yellow hair. Hey, he could be a banana."

Essie clapped her hands. "He would make a perfect banana, but we'll have to ask him. Maybe he won't like that."

"Yeah, maybe everybody will want to eat him. I can't wait to tell him."

"Why don't you ask Joey to come over tomorrow after school, and we can talk about it? He can stay for supper, and we'll take him home later."

"Yeah! Can we have pizza? Please, Mama," Jamie begged.

"Yes, you can have pizza. Do you have homework?"

"I just have to finish reading my story."

"You go do that, then we're having that good rice hot dish you like."

"Yum!" Jamie stuck his tongue out and licked his lips as he ran to get his book.

After Essie dropped Jamie at school the next day, she went up to her room and opened up Nana's old sewing machine. Hoping it still worked, she found a scrap of material in the drawer and sat. She stepped on the foot pedal, and the old machine came to life.

Overtaken by nostalgia, she could see herself sitting in Nana's lap, guiding a piece of fabric under the presser foot as Nana slowly pushed the pedal. It had been the reason she'd talked her mother into buying her a sewing machine as she got older. She was no expert, but she could put together a simple garment without too many problems. She smiled as she thought of her next project, a carrot and a banana.

Essie had just returned from *Uncle Ziggy's Pizza* when Lark dropped the boys off. He stuck his head in the door. "Just making sure this is okay with you, and not just something these two little connivers thought up on their own."

"No, it's a genuine invitation. In fact, it was my idea. This is our Halloween costume planning party." As always, Essie's heart gave an extra beat when she saw him. She motioned for him to come in, and he stepped inside.

"Oh." He released a big gulp of air through his lips. "Thanks for the reprieve. Halloween's not one of my favorite fatherly duties."

"Then you don't mind if I make Joey's costume, do you? We have a few ideas."

Lark whistled in relief. "I'd be delighted. I'll pay you for any materials you use."

"Mama," Jamie said, "we could ask Mr. Winters to stay for supper. He likes pizza, remember?"

She did indeed remember as it was her first encounter with Diana.

"No, Jamie, I wouldn't want to crash your party," Lark said.

"You're welcome to stay. I got a large, so there's plenty." Essie knew it would be uncomfortable, but she needed to get used to it.

"Please, Daddy, you can help us plan," Joey said. "I'm gonna be a banana, and Jamie a carrot."

"A banana! Come to think of it, you do sort of look like a banana," Lark teased.

Essie smiled. She enjoyed watching the loving reaction between this father and son, one she hoped she portrayed with Jamie.

"Please, Mr. Winters. Mama don't mind, do you?" Jamie asked hopefully.

"No, Mr. Winters is welcome to stay if he would like," Essie said.

Lark looked at Essie and shook his head from side to side. "And to think, I have them both together, all day long. It does smell good, though."

"Yeah!" the boys cheered, both clapping their hands.

"I really do appreciate your help with Joey's costume," Lark said.

"That's okay, 'cause Joey don't have no mama to make him

one like me," Jamie said proudly.

"I'm sorry," Essie said when the boys went upstairs. "Jamie shouldn't have said that."

"Don't worry about it. He was just stating a fact. Besides, Joey didn't miss a bite of pizza. So you're a seamstress, too, among all your other talents."

"Oh yeah, I can whip up a mean banana and carrot." She laughed.

"I usually take Joey and Jamie trick-or-treating on Halloween. We go to a few of the neighbor's houses. Would you like to walk along with us this year, or do you have other plans with Jamie? It will be the Sunday before Halloween."

"I'd love to," Essie said. "It'll be fun to see all the kids in their costumes. It was always one of my favorite holidays." There was that familiar heartbeat again.

The boys came running down from upstairs. "Daddy, can I spend the night with Jamie? We gotta finish planning our costumes."

Essie and Lark looked at each other, amazed at the excuses the boys would come up with to be with each other.

"How much planning does a banana and carrot take?" Lark asked

Joey shrugged with an *I got caught* look on his face.

"Not tonight. It's a school night. Get your coat. It's almost bedtime. Tell Miss Essie thank you for the pizza."

"Thank you for the pizza and my banana." Joey giggled.

"Come on, little banana. Time to go." Lark helped Joey zip his jacket.

The rest of that week was a busy one for her. She went shopping for material and found yellow and orange with a little green for the trim on Jamie's carrot. She measured the boys, sewed the costumes, and like a proud mother, took a lot of pictures. Somewhere in all the activity, she found time to call

Martha. She let her know she thought her idea was wonderful, and she was on board to save Miss Ida's house. They set a meeting date to discuss their views, each vowing to recruit as many people as they could.

On Thursday, the boys wore their costumes to school. Afterwards, when Jamie got home, he told Essie all about the party and how the kids were dressed.

"And me and Joey was the best ones there. Everybody wanted to eat us, except Tommy. He said he didn't like carrots."

"Well, I love carrots, and I'm sure Tommy would, too, if he would just try them." Essie rumpled his hair. "You go change clothes and bring your costume to me. Looks like ketchup. Who ever heard of putting ketchup on carrots? I'll have to wash this before we go trick-or-treating."

At church on Sunday, Lark told Essie he would be at her house with Joey at about five-thirty. Jamie was so excited she had to make him sit and eat a few bites of the soup she'd warmed for him.

It was a chilly night, but thankfully, Essie had made the costumes big enough to fit the boy's coats underneath. She went to the closet and took out the orange cap she'd bought as a surprise for Jamie. She'd woven some green leaves from an old flower arrangement she'd found in the attic onto the cap's tassel. She pulled the cap on and led him to the mirror.

"And now, my little carrot, you are ready to go."

Jamie grinned. "I'm a carrot top, just like Grandma said."

When Joey arrived, he was as excited as Jamie. The boys took off down the street as Essie and Lark hurried to keep up with them.

"I should have warned you to wear your running shoes," Lark said.

"You asked me if I wanted to walk along. This is more like working out at the gym."

Stopping at the houses with outside lights on, Lark reminded them, "Be sure and say thank you." They stood back and watched as the boys boldly marched up and rang the doorbells.

At one house, an older lady commented, "What a nice little family you are. I bet you're twins, aren't you?"

Joey shook his head shyly. "No, ma'am, but I wish we was."

"He's my bestest friend in the whole wide world," Jamie said.

The lady laughed. "I guess being bestest friends is almost as good as being twins." She waved to Lark and Essie.

As the boys ran ahead, Lark looked at Essie and grinned. "How does it feel, being called a married mom with twin boys?"

A broad smile crossed her face. "I wouldn't mind twins at all if they were anything like those two."

"Unlikely twins. A redhead and a blond. But we would make a good-looking family, don't you think?" He looked steadily at her.

She blushed. "I think we better get back."

"It's time to head back. I promised Mrs. Pearson I would bring you to her house," Lark said as they caught up with the boys.

"Oh, goody! Can Jamie come, too? She always gives me a big bag. She said she makes it special for me 'cause I'm special. And then can we go to Mrs. Jordan's. She just lives over by the school. She told us all to come so she could see our costumes."

"No, I think you have enough sugar in that bag to drive me crazy for a whole week," Lark said with a laugh.

"You take the boys to Mrs. Pearson's, and I'll head back

and fix us a snack," Essie said. "I don't know about Joey, but Jamie needs some good solid food before he starts on that bag of candy."

"Not a bad idea. We'll be back in about half an hour. Come on, boys." Lark led the boys to his truck and buckled their seat belts, and they left.

When Essie got home, she went directly to the freezer and took out a bag of chicken wings, corn, and French fries. She knew the fries weren't the healthiest thing on the menu, but maybe the grease would coat their stomachs. Silly, she didn't know where she'd heard that, but at least it was something the boys would eat.

Lark and the boys returned, their plastic pumpkins full, to the delicious scent of chicken and French fries.

"Smells wonderful," Lark said as he helped the boys off with their coats.

"Everything will be ready in fifteen minutes," Essie said as she took their coats from Lark and threw them on a nearby chair.

They followed Essie into the kitchen where Lark sat at the table and gestured for the boys to sit. "Just enough time to check your goodies." He patted the empty spot in front of each of them. "Everything on the table."

The boys poured their candy out, careful to keep their piles separate.

"Wow! Look at all this good stuff. I'll take one of these and two of these." Lark grabbed three big candy bars and pulled them toward him. "Essie, come look at all this good candy. Better come pick out your share before they eat it all up," he teased.

"Aw, Daddy, you're getting the bestest kind," Joey whined.

"Okay." Lark pouted. "If you don't want me to have any, I guess I'll just have to do without." He wiped a make-believe tear from his eye.

Joey picked out a red sucker and handed it to Lark. "You can have this one. I have lots of these."

"Oh goody, my favorite." He made a funny face at Joey and stuck the sucker in his pocket.

Watching them from afar, Essie recalled her dad doing the same thing to her and how she treasured those memories. Lark really was a wonderful father to Joey. If only she could be as wonderful a mother to Jamie.

"I need you to clear the table so we can eat," she called out.

Lark helped the boys put their candy back in their pumpkins, Essie brought the food to the table, and they all ate heartily.

"We're just like a family, like that lady said," Jamie said, looking around the table. "She thought me and Joey was twins, and you and Mr. Winters was our mama and daddy."

Lark cut his eyes over at Essie and quickly looked away. She felt herself blushing.

Lark cleared his throat. "She got it half right. I'm Joey's daddy, and Miss Essie is your mama. Why don't you boys go upstairs and play while I help with the dishes," he said.

"Can we have some candy now? We ate good like you said," Joey reminded him.

"Yes, but go easy on it. Save a few pieces for tomorrow."

Essie got their candy and took them to the table. "You can each pick out three pieces. If you take bigger ones, you only get two. Does that sound fair?"

"That sounds fair to me," Lark said. "Let me see. I'll take this one and this one." He again chose the biggest pieces.

"Daddy!" Joey squealed.

The boy chose their candy and ran upstairs as Essie and Lark started the dishes.

Essie slapped Lark playfully on the arm. "Shame on you teasing Joey like that. Get busy and dry the dishes. You're getting way behind."

Lark laughed. "Yes, dear. Nag, nag. Do the dishes. Take out the garbage. Do you want me to scrub the floor, too?"

Essie picked up the dishtowel and popped him with it. "Yes, that would be nice. The mop is in the closet."

He took a step toward her, then as if gravity was pulling him back, turned quickly, grabbed the dishtowel, and wiped the plate she handed him.

After church the next Sunday, Jamie and Joey came bursting into the church from Sunday school where Essie and Lark stood chatting.

"Daddy, can I go to Jamie's to play. We want to make a fort in his room. Please, Daddy, can I?"

"Did you ask Miss Essie? Maybe she and Jamie have something else to do."

"Please, Mama, can we?" Jamie leaned in against Essie, his eyes pleading as he looked up at her. "We don't have nothin' else to do. We'll just sit at home and be bored."

The two adults looked at each other and burst out laughing.

"How can I say no to that?" Essie said.

The boys jumped up and down and clapped their hands.

"It's a good thing he didn't ask for a horse," he commented with a wide grin on his face.

"I know. But what kind of mother would I be if I made him sit home with me all afternoon and be bored."

"Okay, bud, get your coat, and we'll go home and change clothes and eat, and I'll drop you off."

"I have a pot of vegetable soup made, if you would like to have lunch with us," Essie offered.

"Homemade soup sounds good to me. You're choice, bud, soup or a peanut butter and jelly sandwich?"

"Yum," Joey said, licking his lips.

"Don't you ever feed that kid anything other than peanut butter and jelly?" she asked, shaking her head.

"Of course," he said with a serious frown on his face. "At least once or twice a week we have pizza."

She slapped him across the shoulder. "I'll see you in about half an hour."

Essie ladled the steaming hot soup into bowls, the aroma filling the room and tickling the noses of everyone waiting to sample it. Jamie and Joey ate fast, but their anxiety came to a halt when Essie set a plate of chocolate brownies before them, topped with marshmallows, and coated with rich fudge frosting.

"Tell Miss Essie thanks for the nice lunch," Lark said to Joey when they were excused to go upstairs. "And go to the bathroom and wipe that chocolate smile off your face."

"Thanks, Miss Essie," he said as he ran up the steps with Jamie, wiping his mouth with his hand, then licking his fingers.

Essie and Lark talked casually about the community hall as they did the dishes. It would be a great loss to the community, and did Lark think Matt Simmons would really shut it down, even if it meant no income to him? The subject of Miss Ida's house was avoided.

As they did the last of the dishes, Lark hung the towel on the rack and turned to her. "I know how busy your life has been with the house renovations and all that happened with Miss Ida and Jamie, but now that things have slowed a bit, will you go on another date with me? I like you a lot, Essie. I want to get to know you better."

Her eyes shifted away from him, and she could feel herself stiffening. Cautiously taking his hands in hers, she looked straight into his eyes. "I like you, too, Lark. You must know I do, but I have so much to learn about being a parent. I want to concentrate all my energy on being the best mother I can be to Jamie." She looked cautiously up at him. "Besides, I have a grand old house to save."

He reached up with his thumb and wiped away the tear that trickled down her cheek. "I know you're afraid, but I can help you. I've been in the same situation for seven years. I have tons of experience. We can do this together, except, you know, saving a house." He tweaked her nose.

She hesitated a moment. "Please understand," she pleaded, "if circumstances were different . . . I'm sorry." She let go of his hands and walked to the window.

Following her, he draped his arm loosely over her shoulder. "Just give it some time. I'll be here for you if you need me. You'll be a wonderful mother to Jamie."

She began shaking, and she couldn't hold back the sobs building up inside her any longer.

He drew her gently to him and held her tight. "It's okay. You've been under a lot of stress for an awful long time. Maybe a good cry is just what you need." He gave her a kiss on the forehead.

"I'm sorry," Essie said, wiping the back of her hand across her eyes. "Can we still be friends, even after I've gushed all over your shirt?"

Lark gave her a peck on the cheek. "We'll always be friends. Are you okay now?"

"Yes, thank you for understanding."

"I need to go now. Tell Joey I'll pick him up about four."

Essie went to the bathroom and washed her face. Was she wrong by turning down a date with Lark? And would he ever ask her out again? The one thing her mother had never told her, and she was learning all by herself, was how much love could hurt.

Lark's heart was wounded, but he would be patient. This beautiful, vibrant lady from Oklahoma was worth waiting for. She'd captured his heart like no one since his wife, Jane. As he parked in front of his house, his cell phone rang. It was Diana, in a state of hysteria. "Calm down. I can't understand a word you are saying," he said to her.

"It's Jim, He came here drinking, and I'm afraid he'll come back. I'm scared, Lark. He threatened me."

"Are you okay? Did he hurt you?" Lark asked anxiously.

"I'm okay. He didn't touch me, but if he keeps drinking, I don't trust him. I'm sorry to bother you. I know you told me to start standing up for myself, but I didn't know what else to do."

"You did the right thing. I told you I'd be there for you if you needed me. Here's what I want you to do. Lock your door and pack a bag. I'll come get you. I don't want you driving here in case he's lurking around somewhere."

"I think he may still have a key to the front door."

"Then jam a chair under the doorknob. I'm leaving now. I'll be there in twenty minutes. If he knocks, just don't answer the door."

When he got there, she threw herself into his arms. "I've never been so glad to see anyone in my life."

Lark could feel her trembling. "Let's get out of here. What he doesn't need is to see his wife with another man. And what I don't need is to be made into meatballs. I'm not a fighting man." He grinned at her.

Diana had calmed down by the time they got back to Lark's. As she settled herself in the spare bedroom, Lark made tea. "Have you had any action from your realtor on your house? I believe now is the time you should think seriously about moving into town where you'll be safe. You're rather isolated out there. I worry about you."

"As a matter of fact, I do. There's this older couple who

have looked at it twice. The realtor expects an offer from them soon."

"Good. How about I get a crew together and move you. I know you've downsized, so my truck should be able to handle most of the furniture."

"You'd do that for me?"

Lark noticed the surprised expression on her face. "Of course! Diana, you're not alone. You have lots of friends, including me, who are willing to help."

"I'm thinking about those apartments by the school. I'll check with them on Monday."

"It's all set then. You get your apartment rented, and I'll start working on it. Now to other business, I'm picking up Joey at four at Essie's. You ride along with me, and we'll stop at the grocery store. My pantry isn't exactly up to par." He smiled at her. "You decide what you want to eat, then you can cook it for me."

She smiled back at him. "How about that Chinese noodle dish you and Joey like so much?"

At four o'clock, Essie, in the middle of an Old Maid game of cards with the boys, heard Lark's truck as he parked in front of her house. A quick glance outside and her heart sank to an all-time low as she saw Lark exit and Diana waiting on the passenger side. He certainly had wasted no time in running back to her.

"Thank Miss Essie for having you over," he said to Joey as he helped him with his jacket. "And for the *Kool-Aid* I see around your mouth."

"Thank you," he said as he wiped his sleeve across his mouth.

She gave Joey a hug and walked him to the door. "You're welcome here anytime, Joey."

Essie glanced toward the truck, then at Lark. He hesitated, then, with his hand on Joey's back, hurried him out the door.

Essie's brain tried hard to unscramble the meaning behind what had happened earlier while lying awake for hours that night. How could Lark ask her to go out with him and four hours later show up at her house with Diana? Did he do this on purpose? Was he trying to make her jealous, or had he just simply given up on her? Becoming more determined than ever to stick to the goals she'd laid out for herself, being a good mother to Jamie, and saving Miss Ida's house, Essie finally fell asleep.

Chapter Ten

Essie chuckled quietly to herself as she headed up to Jamie's room to quiet the boys. Joey was spending the night, and she'd put them to bed an hour ago, but they were still chattering away. She stopped by the door and listened.

"If Miss Essie and Daddy loved each other, we would be like a family. Then we could sleep together all the time," she heard Joey say.

"Yeah, but they'd have to be married before we'd be a family."

"Yeah, and if they married, we'd be brothers. We'd be like twins like that lady said, 'cause we're both seven. And we'd have to wear the same kind of clothes 'cause twins always do that." They both giggled.

"Maybe they will, 'cause they like each other. I can tell 'cause they always laugh when they say something funny," Jamie replied.

Essie smothered her giggle as she listened to these two little characters plotting to get her and Lark together.

"But it has to be a lot. Like they have to be in love. I mean really, really, really a lot."

"Yeah, like kissing and everything." She almost choked, trying to hold her laughter back. *When did these two little boys get so smart?*

"Boy, that'd be cool," Joey said. "You and me both would have a mama and daddy just like everybody else."

"And live in the same house and get our lessons together. We'd be the smartest ones in our class. And we'd have our teacher to help us if we didn't know how."

"And we could have lots of cookies 'cause your mama is always baking."

Like they don't already have enough.

"We could ask her, and she'd let us help her. Remember when we made them snickerdoodles?"

"Everybody at school loved them. And remember, we told them we made them all by ourselves," Joey said. They both giggled.

Little stinkers. What else had they been saying at school, she wondered.

"Maybe if we make them see each other a lot, they'll get in love. But we have to let them be by theirselves, 'cause they won't do it in front of us," Jamie said, plotting.

"When my daddy comes to your house, let's always come up to your room. Then they can kiss and do all that stuff without us seeing them."

Essie turned quickly and went back downstairs, muffling her laughter with her hand. Here these two little seven-year-olds were plotting to get her and Lark together, and there she was, trying her very best to keep from falling further in love with him.

To the delight of both boys, three inches of snow had fallen during the night. Breakfast was rapidly devoured, enhanced by their plans to make the *bestest snowman* ever. Essie helped them get into their coats, gloves, hats, and boots and assisted them as they hustled outside.

As she watched through the window, it brought back memories of the times she and her parents had visited her nana at Christmas. She remembered her dad helping her roll the big snowballs and stacking them to make a giant snowman. In her mind, Essie could see her nana taking the scarf from her own neck and gently wrapping it around the snowman's neck. The funny straw hat that always hung on a nail on the back porch gave their perfect creation its finishing touches.

Essie went to the closet and found a bright-colored scarf, took the orange cap Jamie wore for Halloween, and put on her coat and gloves. Looking around the room, she spotted some small stones she'd placed in a saucer around a candle.

She grabbed a handful for the eyes and mouth and stuck them in her pocket, then went to the refrigerator and located a small carrot. Hurrying to join the boys outside, she vowed to make this the *bestest snowman* in the whole neighborhood.

Struggling to lift one big snowball onto the other, she and the boys turned to see Pete parked in front of the house. A chill ran down Essie's spine, remembering the last time she'd seen the truck.

"Mr. Pete!" the boys both hollered as they ran to give him a hug.

"We're making a big, giant snowman," Joey said.

"Kind of looks like you need some help." Pete flexed his muscles.

"Mama said we should of made it in one piece 'cause then we wouldn't have to lift it," Jamie said.

"Yeah, but we like rolling the big balls up. They get bigger and bigger, but we had to make one bigger than the other," Joey explained. "And then we have to make a little one for his head."

Pete winked at Essie, took the snowball, and grunting as if he could hardly lift it, hoisted it on top of the larger one. "All we need now is a head."

Joey and Jamie ran off to find clean snow to make the head. Grinning at her, Pete reached to get a handful of snow and packed it into a ball.

"You wouldn't dare," Essie said, forgetting all about her last encounter with Pete. She turned and ran, veering from left to right, but Pete's aim was too good. He hit her square between the shoulders with the snowball.

"You're in for it now because I'm declaring an all-out war!" Essie proclaimed. "Come on, boys, let's go get Mr. Pete."

The boys came running, packing the snow into small balls as they ran. The three of them pelted Pete from all sides.

Pete fell back into the snow. "No more, please. I give up." The boys piled on top of him, wrestling until they all lay exhausted. "We better do something about this headless snowman," Pete said, out of breath. The boys ran off to finish rolling the ball they had started.

When it was done, they all stood back and agreed it was the *darn bestest snowman* in town. They christened him Mr. Popsicle.

"Let's make snow angels all around Mr. Popsicle so they can protect him," Jamie said.

"Yeah, that way, he won't never melt." Joey plopped down in the snow.

As the boys played, Pete whispered in Essie's ear, "I need to talk to you . . . alone."

Suddenly, Essie felt herself stiffen. Had he seen her at the Sawyer farm? Maybe he wanted to explain what he was doing there, what kind of deal he was making. Or maybe he needed to know how much she knew.

"We can go inside and have a cup of coffee," Essie said. "Jamie, you and Joey stay close. Joey's daddy will be here soon."

Seated at the table inside, Essie poured Pete a cup of coffee and sat down across from him. "What's up, Doc?" she asked casually.

He took her hand. "I don't want you to worry because probably nothing will ever come of it."

She gasped heavily. "You're scaring me, Pete. What is it?"

He hesitated a moment. "I got a call from Rod Sheffield,

Miss Ida's lawyer, this morning. Her son Robert is in town. He was asking about Jamie."

Her heart pounded frantically, and she suddenly felt woozy. "What did he want? Is he going to try and take Jamie from me? I won't let him. He has no rights." She pounded the table with her fist.

Pete got up, came around the table, and laid his hand on her trembling fist. "You're correct. He has no rights. He gave them up when Miss Ida adopted Jamie." He put his arm around her shoulder. "You need to calm down. We don't want you getting all upset over this."

"But is there any way he can get around that? It happens all the time." She pulled her hand away and jumped to her feet.

"Rod says the only reason he's interested in Jamie is because his mother left all her money to him. He doesn't want Jamie or the responsibility that goes with it. You can bet on that."

"Where was he when his mother was sick?" Essie asked. "That money is for Jamie and his education. If Miss Ida had wanted her son to have her money, she would have left it to him." She wiped a tear from her cheek.

"Rod just wanted you to know he was in town, in case he bothered you. He made it quite clear that everything's proper and legal on paper. There's no way he can get custody of Jamie."

"What about the money? It rightfully belongs to Jamie," Essie said.

"He can contest the will, which Rod says he has a right to do. There isn't much chance of him ever getting a penny of it, though," Pete said.

"I'll give him every penny of that money if I have to, but I want him to stay away from Jamie. What if he tries to see him?" Essie shivered.

"We'll just have to make sure he doesn't." He took her hand and squeezed it.

"But I don't even know what he looks like. What if he shows up at school?" She could feel herself starting to shake again.

"We'll have Lark watch over Jamie. There will be someone with him at all times."

Essie looked out the window at Jamie, so happy and carefree, and couldn't imagine her life without him. She wouldn't be completely satisfied until she'd adopted him, a process she intended to start very soon.

Lark came for Joey shortly after Pete left. The boys were still busy making their snow angels, so Essie motioned Lark inside. "I need to talk to you."

"Oh no, I'll clean up his mess, I'll replace what he broke, and give him a good lecture if you promise not to take him to court," Lark teased.

"Oh shush, this is serious." Essie slapped him on the arm. "Sit down, and I'll get you a cup of coffee."

"I'm serious. He's a disaster at times."

"Rod Sheffield called Pete this morning," Essie said. "Miss Ida's son is in town."

"Whoa, that can't be good." Lark wiped the smile from his face. "How does Rod know he's here?"

"He came to see Rod. He was asking about Jamie."

"More like, he was asking about the money, I bet," Lark said with a scoff.

"Yes. Get to Jamie, get to the money. Rod assured us there was nothing Robert could do to get custody of Jamie. He said he might contest the will."

"So where do you go from here? You don't think he'll try to see Jamie, do you?" he asked.

"I'm afraid he will," Essie admitted. "That's why I wanted to ask you if you would keep an eye on Jamie at school." She stared at him hopefully.

"You know I will. We have a little routine every morning about not talking to anyone they don't know. It's sort of a game we play."

"I've talked to him also about talking to strangers. I wonder if Jamie even knows his dad? I don't want to scare him, but right now, I'm not going to let him out of my sight."

Ambling over to the window, Essie felt a cold chill run through her body as her eyes scanned the yard for the boys. As she walked closer, she caught a glimpse of them hunched down below the window, peeking in. The two little imps were spying on her and Lark. She put her hand over her mouth, took a deep breath, and turned back to face Lark.

"The snow is so nice and fluffy. I was thinking about taking them to the park and letting them ride their saucers," Lark said. "What do you think? Would you like to go?"

"I don't know. It's such a public place. What if we see Robert there? I don't even know what he looks like."

Lark took her by both arms and pulled her to him. "You can't let yourself get paranoid over this. We'll be with him every minute."

As Essie looked over Lark's shoulder, she could see four happy little eyes watching them. She felt a tug at her heart as she pushed herself away from him.

Delighted to be going to the park, the boys kept busy the rest of the morning. Amidst the chaos of finding dry mittens, running between the two houses, finding their saucers, and eating lunch, they finally left in Lark's truck.

Excitement ran high as they unloaded their saucers and trudged through the deep snow. The small incline, located away from the larger slope, was designated especially for the younger and more cautious beginners. The boys jumped on their saucers, and Lark gave them a slow push. Down the little hill they went, squealing and laughing. Picking up their saucers, the boys labored back up for another ride.

On one of the trips down, Jamie's saucer skipped out of the rut and overturned, dumping him in the soft, fluffy snow. He crawled up laughing, and Essie laughed with him until she saw a man she didn't recognize walking toward him. At once, her laughter died away.

"Oh no," Essie said as she started down the hill, her heart pumping wildly.

Lark grabbed her by the hand and stopped her. "It's okay," he said. "That's one of my student's dads. He's just making sure Jamie isn't hurt."

Regardless of how hard she tried, Essie couldn't put her uneasiness to rest. Wherever she went, she was aware of every movement around her. Her eyes constantly checking out any man she didn't know. When she dropped Jamie off at school the next morning, she watched until he was inside the building. At the grocery store, she checked every man standing in the checkout line, and on the rare occasion when a lone male walked the sidewalk in front of her house, she watched him until he was out of sight.

On Monday morning, she went to see Rod Sheffield and had him start the process of adoption. As she sat filling out papers, her date of birth was required, and she realized she'd forgotten about her birthday, which was only a week away. Since her parents had died, each year had passed quietly without the fuss her mother had always made over her. This year, she decided she deserved a real celebration with her friends and her son at her side.

"I have a birthday next week, and I think we'll have a big party. What do you think?" she asked Jamie when he came home from school.

"Yeah, I like birthday parties. Can Joey come, and can we

have some yummy cake?" Jamie's face lit up. "Can Joey's daddy come, too? You like him, don't you? Parties are for people you like a whole bunch." He spread his hands far apart.

She smiled. "Yes, they both can come. And Mr. Pete, too."

"Yea! I can't wait to tell Joey."

It didn't take long for the news to spread. Lark and Pete both insisted the party should be at Trevor's. They all agreed on Sunday at five-thirty. The next day Jamie was excited to tell Essie all the new things he'd learned about the rules of giving your own birthday party.

"'Cause Mr. Winters said you can't cook on your birthday, and Mr. Pete said whoever heard of anybody making their own birthday cake." Jamie took a deep breath. "And Mr. Pete told me I better gussy up, and I gotta get you a present and wrap it." He fell over on the sofa. "Boy, these birthday parties sure are hard work."

Essie tickled him. "Just wait until your birthday. It'll be the biggest one you have ever had. Now go change your clothes because I have a special snack for you today."

"Oh boy, what is it?" Jamie asked.

"I won't tell you. You change out of your school clothes first, then you'll see."

He jumped up and ran up the stairs.

On Wednesday, Pete told Essie that he and Jamie had something to do and that he was picking him up after school.

"It's a secret, and I can't tell you, 'cause then it wouldn't be a secret," Jamie said.

It was almost time for supper when Pete brought Jamie home. Essie could see them talking and giggling as Jamie grasped the package Pete handed him.

Once inside, hiding the bag behind him, Jamie sidled to the stairway, then ran up the steps, hollering as he went. "I have to change my clothes!"

Pete winked at Essie. "My, what a thoughtful child you have."

Essie called up the stairs. "Did you thank Mr. Pete for doing whatever your secret was?"

"Thank you, Mr. Pete!" Jamie hollered from upstairs.

"You're welcome," Pete said. "I'll see you at church Sunday. And don't forget to gussy up." He grinned at Essie.

"Get out of here," she said. "And quit teaching my son your street language."

On Thursday, Essie asked Pete if he could watch Jamie while she met with some of the girls. Fairly sure that Lark had already talked to Pete about the rec center, and not wanting to put him in the position of taking sides, Essie didn't tell him the true reason for the meeting.

Six ladies, most of them friends of Martha's, showed up for the meeting. Only Mrs. Dawson, whom Essie had picked up was her recruit.

"Looks like it may be women against the men on this thing," Martha said, looking around the room.

"And most likely, parents, too. I can understand what a good thing this would be for the young people. I just don't think it should be at the expense of Miss Ida's house," Essie said.

"We'll have to show them the power of women," Martha said. "I've been looking into this, and there's one thing we can do, and I think we should do it right away. We should apply to get it on the National Historical Registry. If we can accomplish that, we'll have their hands tied."

"That may seem kind of like a dirty way to fight, but I'm all for it," one lady said and laughed.

Everyone agreed. "I don't think they'll be doing anything soon anyway, even if it goes the other way. They have no money," another lady added. "They'll have to plan all kinds of fundraisers."

"I think that's about all we can do right now, but keep talking to your friends, to your husbands, and to anyone who will listen, and recruit, recruit, recruit," Martha said.

"How do we go about this?" Essie asked. "If I can be of any help, just let me know."

"Working in the mayor's office, I have all the connections we need. I'll get started on it right away." Martha winked at the ladies. "What do you say, we keep this kind of quiet for now?"

"Might be a good idea," Mrs. Dawson said.

Sunday morning after church, excitement filled the air as Jamie and Essie got ready for her party. Essie couldn't decide what to wear. Finally, she narrowed it down to a tan pantsuit, a blue princess-style dress, or a red jersey dress that draped softly around her body. She recalled the occasion she'd bought the red dress. It was after one of her quarrels with Brad and her friend Emma had just broken up with her boyfriend. They went out and bought what they, in their conservative minds, considered rather provocative outfits, and went out on the town.

"Jamie, come help Mama pick out what to wear," Essie said.

Jamie's eyes lit up as he saw the red dress laid out on the bed. "Wear that one." He pointed to the red. "You'll be the prettiest mama in the whole wide world."

Why not? she thought. It was her birthday. She had cause to celebrate how her life had changed in the last few months. She had Nana's house back in order, had a wonderful son, and good friends. What more could she ask for? She put on the red dress and was ready when Pete stopped by to pick them up.

"Wow, you look fantastic," Pete said.

"Thank you. You don't think it's too much?" she asked as she danced around in front of him.

"It's perfect. You're beautiful." Pete pulled her close and gave her a friendly peck on the cheek.

"That's 'cause I picked out the prettiest dress Mama has." Jamie put his hands on his hips and puffed out his chest.

"You did a great job, and you look pretty spiffy yourself," Pete said.

"I'm all gussied up like you told me." He grinned up at Pete.

When they got to Trevor's, they were shown to a private room where Lark and Joey were already seated. The table was set with beautiful china and a centerpiece of red roses. A big banner with *Happy Birthday* stretched across one wall.

"Happy birthday!" they all called out as Essie entered the door. Pete took her coat, and Lark stood and pulled out the chair beside him, while the boys smothered their giggles behind their hands.

Lark leaned over and whispered, "You look beautiful."

After a great dinner and with the table cleared, Pete excused himself and came back with the waitress carrying a birthday cake topped with lighted candles. Another server followed with plates, forks, and a serving knife.

They all clapped and hollered, "Happy birthday!"

"Let's all sing," Pete said, swinging his hands like a conductor. Joining their voices in a melodic chorus, they belted out their version of the usual tune.

"Blow out the candles, Mama, but first you got to make a wish, but don't tell us 'cause then it won't come true," Jamie instructed.

"What more could I wish for than what I already have?" Essie took Jamie's hand. "I might need some help blowing, though."

They blew hard, and all the candles flickered and went out. "Mama, look! You're only ten years old 'cause you only got ten candles."

"Wow! I'm only three years older than you. Guess they didn't want to start a fire, so they didn't put all thirty-two on," Essie said

"We got to give you our presents now. You have to open mine first," Jamie said.

"What? I have a cake and presents, too?" Essie raised her brow and tucked her chin in.

"You always have to have presents for your birthday," Jamie said. "Me and Mr. Pete went shopping. That was our secret. We fooled you." He giggled and put his hand over his mouth.

"You sure did. I thought you were sneaking off to have pizza without me."

Jamie handed her a small, wrapped package.

"I wonder what this is. It sort of feels like a handkerchief."

"No, you'll never guess in a million years, Mama. Just open it."

Essie tore the paper and pulled out a pair of black leather gloves. "Thank you, sweetheart. Just what I needed. But how did you know what I was going to wish for when I blew out my candles?"

"I didn't know." Jamie looked surprised. "I guess me and Mr. Pete must be pretty smart," he said.

Essie winked at Pete as she drew her son close and gave him a kiss. "I think you're two of the smartest people I know."

Joey handed her a package. "This is from Daddy and me." He stood by, watching her unwrap it.

"Thank you," she said as she opened the box. It was a plain white blouse. She turned it around, and on the back was written, *Proud to be a Mama.*

She gave Joey a hug. "I *am* proud to be a mama, and

especially to you," she said to Jamie as she kissed him on his forehead. "Thank you, guys. I'll wear it proudly."

"The roses are from me," Pete said. "Don't forget to take them home with you."

"I won't. What a wonderful birthday. Thanks to all of you."

As Pete and the boys loaded up the roses, the rest of the cake, and presents, Lark walked her to Pete's SUV. She felt the electricity as he placed his hand on her back.

"I've never seen you look more gorgeous. Red is definitely your color. You should wear it more often," Lark said.

"I always feel a little daring when I wear red, but Jamie picked it out and insisted it was the one."

Lark stopped and faced her. "Essie, you know how I . . ."

"All loaded up and ready to go!" Pete called to her.

"Coming," Essie called back. "I have to go. Thanks again for everything," she said to Lark.

What was Lark trying to say when they'd been interrupted? All these questions flooded her mind. Had she been wrong about him and Diana? Did he really feel she didn't care about the needs of the youth, and would this thing about Miss Ida's house come between them? She wondered if he would ever ask her out again, and if he did, would she go? Confused more than ever, she wondered if she'd taken on more than she could handle.

Picking out a birthday gift for Essie took a lot of thought and reasoning from Lark. He wanted a meaningful gift for her, yet not something he wanted to share with everyone. After hours of thinking about it, he chose the plain white blouse with an obvious caption on its back. But as something to be shared just between the two of them, he slipped a small package into the pocket, one that held the contents of his heart. He'd picked this night to tell her exactly how he felt, but just as he began, they'd been interrupted. If Jane could know, he believed she would approve. But something was holding Essie back. Was it Diana? His hands were tied. He'd made a promise, and no matter how trivial, he wouldn't break it because it was important to Diana. And this thing about Miss Ida's house. Other than a few awkward moments between them, no problem had occurred, but how did she really feel about it? But more importantly, how did she feel about him?

Marching through the new snow that was beginning to fall, Pete and Jamie unloaded everything from the vehicle into the house. Essie cut and wrapped a large piece of cake for Pete. Jamie was yawning by the time Pete left, so Essie put him to bed and changed into her pajamas and Nana's cozy robe.

While she was reflecting on the events of the evening, her thoughts were interrupted by the chiming of the doorbell. Her mind, refusing to forget the pleasures of the day, she thought perhaps Lark had returned to complete the conversation he'd left unfinished. With an air of expectancy, she leaped from the sofa and opened the door.

Standing before her was a rather tall man dressed in jeans and a dark-colored parka, the hood pulled over his head. She froze as she noticed a mop of long red hair, just the exact color of Jamie's, sticking out from underneath his hood.

Her knees were weak, her voice trembling, but she spoke quickly, "Excuse me, but I need to turn off a burner on my stove. I'll be right back." She closed the door slowly and quietly slid the bolt into place. Hurrying into the kitchen, she grabbed her cell phone and called Pete.

"Robert Sands is at my door," she whispered when Pete answered.

"What!" Pete yelled into the phone. "Are you sure? How do you know it's him?"

"He has red hair just like Jamie's. I know it's him." She shook all over.

"Don't you dare open that door. I'm on my way. Stay on the phone."

Essie, cowering in a corner away from all windows, whispered into the phone, "Where are you now? Please hurry."

"I'm on my way. Where are you?"

"I'm in the kitchen. I told him I had to turn the burner off my stove."

"You talked to him!" Pete yelled at her. "Are your doors locked? I can't believe you opened the door."

"My door's bolted. I thought it was you or Lark. Please hurry, I'm so scared. How far away are you?" she asked.

"I'm just coming around the corner. I see him on your porch. I'm hanging up. You stay put until I tell you to open the door," he instructed.

Her racing heart calmed somewhat, only to be replaced by the fear she had for Pete's safety. She pulled herself up from the floor where she was huddled and went to the parlor. Walking quietly to the bay window, she pulled the heavy drape back into a small peephole. She could see Pete jump out of his truck and walk cautiously toward the front porch.

Essie watched closely as the big man turned to Pete. She quickly unlocked the window and raised it a tiny bit so she could hear their conversation.

"What are you doing here?" Pete asked brusquely.

"I'm waiting for the lady who lives here. I have business with her." The man stood firmly in place, his feet spread wide apart, as he spoke in a self-assured tone.

"What kind of business?" Pete walked around between the man and the door.

"That's between the lady and me. Who are you?" the big man asked with a tone of authority.

"Let's just say, I'm an interested party. And the lady wants nothing to do with you, so why don't you just go?" Essie could see Pete flinch as the man shifted his stance.

"That lady has my son and a whole lot of money that belongs to me. She better want to see me," he expounded in a threatening way.

"Oh! You mean the son that you gave away and have never paid one penny to help support? And money from your mother, who died without even knowing whether you were dead or alive?"

Essie's heart raced as she took in a silent gulp of air. She marveled at Pete's audacity. Didn't he realize this man could make hamburger of him if he so desired? Yet he kept right on pushing him.

"That's none of your business. It's between me and her." The man looked toward the door expectantly.

"I'm making it my business. You don't want the boy, and Miss Ida left that money where she wanted it. You will never see a penny of it." Pete stared at him, his eyes never wavering.

"We'll see what my lawyer has to say about that," the man said confidently.

Pete chuckled. "Your lawyer, huh? If you want to talk to a lawyer, talk to Rod Sheffield. He'll tell you that your mother has this tied up so tight that a magician couldn't get the knot out. Now, why don't you get out of here and go back to where you came from?"

The big man took a step closer, put his hands on his hips, and stood glaring at Pete. "Oh yeah, we'll just see about that."

Pete straightened his small frame to his full five foot ten, drew in a big gulp of the cold crisp air, and glared back at him. The man returned his gaze, never faltering for a moment.

Suddenly, without another word, the man turned and walked away. Pete hollered after him. "And don't come bothering this lady again." He called out to Essie, "Open the door. He's gone."

Essie pulled herself away from the drape, opened the door, and jumped into Pete's arms. "Are you sure he's gone? I've never been so frightened in my life."

"He's gone." He looked at her sternly. "What were you thinking, opening that door without knowing who was there?"

"I guess I wasn't thinking. I just thought it might be Lark," she muttered meekly.

Pete looked at her and raised his brow. "So, you were expecting Lark?"

"Not really, but he started to tell me something tonight, and he never finished. I just thought maybe it was him."

Pete rolled his eyes at her. "Or, more like hoping."

She grinned slyly. "You sure pushed that guy hard. I was afraid he'd hit you. Weren't you scared?"

"Mr. Pete, scared? Are you kidding?" Suddenly he wrinkled his brow. "Wait a minute. Were you listening?"

She grinned. "I opened the window a crack. I wanted to cheer you on in case he challenged you to a duel."

"Awful brave of you, hiding behind a window. If it'd been you, I would've come out with a baseball bat. Anyway, I don't think he will be bothering you again."

"But what if you're wrong? What if he comes back tonight?"

"Get me a pillow and blanket. I'm staying right here on your sofa." He shook his head. "I can't believe after being so careful all this time, you opened your door without knowing who was there," he scolded.

"Why do you think he won't come back? Did Mr. Pete put the scare into him?" she teased.

"He doesn't want Jamie, and he knows he doesn't have a chance of getting any of that money. Besides, he had that defeated look on his face." Pete looked at her and grinned. Raising his arms up and flexing his muscles, he said, "He doesn't want to mess with Mr. Pete."

CHAPTER ELEVEN

Nothing could shut down Rosepoint faster than eight inches of snow. The school was closed, activities were canceled, and many of the smaller businesses hadn't bothered to open their doors. A little more than a week remained until Thanksgiving. The children were delighted to be out of school, along with the deer hunters who were hoping for better tracking conditions made possible with the new fallen snow. Sudden gusts of ice-cold wind could easily send someone reeling in a different direction if they weren't alert. One wouldn't venture far without a warm scarf tied tightly around their face, and they were blinded by steamy glasses the minute they stepped into a warm room. It was winter at its worse, and Essie had never seen anything like it.

Although the weather had suddenly become harsh, Essie looked forward to Thanksgiving. She closed her eyes and could smell the sweet aroma of cinnamon and nutmeg as the apple and pumpkin pies were taken from the oven and set on racks to cool. She could almost taste the savory turkey, browned to perfection with lots and lots of gravy, and the smell of sage wafting heavily in the air as the stuffing was scooped from its insides. She sighed at the idea that there would only be the three of them for Thanksgiving. Lark's parents were coming, and he and Joey were taking them to Trevor's.

She hadn't heard or seen any more of Robert Sands. Although their close surveillance around Jamie hadn't loosened, she began to relax and believed Pete had been right.

The more she thought about Thanksgiving, the more nostalgic she became. Her first Thanksgiving in Nana's house couldn't be minimized by anything on her table other than the traditional turkey dinner, even if there were only three of them. She sat down and wrote out her menu. Then she made a list of what she would need from the grocery store. Since Jamie and Joey were out sledding with Pete, she decided it was time to do her shopping.

She couldn't help but notice the strategically placed poster calling for the backing for a rec center in Miss Ida's house. It seemed Lark and his boys had been busy. It reminded her to call Martha to see what was happening with their proposal.

The store was busier than normal. She was searching among the turkeys, trying to find the smallest one, when her hand touched another, reaching for the same turkey. She looked up, mouth agape, to see Lark standing there with her turkey in his hand, grinning down at her.

"This what you're looking for?" Lark held up the turkey.

"Actually, I need one about the size of a Cornish hen."

"I don't think you'll find one that small. If you do, let me know, and I'll take this one."

"Are you really looking for a turkey? I thought you were taking your parents to Trevor's."

"It was my intention. I guess I waited too long to make a reservation. I had no idea it would be so booked up."

"And you're going to cook for your parents? Does your mom know?" Essie's lips curled into a smile as she pictured a peanut butter sandwich with a side order of pizza.

"How hard can it be? You stick it in a pan and let it bake."

Essie nodded her head. "And would you mind sharing the rest of your menu with me?"

"Haven't gotten that far yet. Maybe you can tell me what to buy? Mom can help me cook." He put his palms together in a prayer position. "Please."

"You invite your parents to dinner and then make your mom cook it. I have a better idea. You all come to my house and let me do the cooking."

Lark shook his head. "I couldn't do that."

"Why not? Then I can get a real turkey instead of that Cornish hen you have there."

"But it's so much work. It's my fault. I should have called Trevor's sooner."

"How hard can it be? I'll just stick it in a pan and let it bake." She grinned at him. "I won't take no for an answer."

Lark whistled a sigh of relief and smiled. "Only if you let me buy the turkey."

"Deal. Now let's find a bird with a little meat on its bones." They rummaged through the turkeys until they found the right size and put it in her cart.

Lark followed her along the aisles as she filled her cart. He paid for the turkey and helped her load the bags into the trunk of her car.

Essie spread her hand toward the bags of fresh vegetables and many other items she'd purchased. "You really were going to cook Thanksgiving dinner for your parents?" she said sarcastically.

He shrugged, smiled at her, and slammed the trunk closed. "Do you want me to follow you home and help you unload?"

As soon as she got her groceries put away, she called Martha at the mayor's office. "Hi Martha, this is Essie Euller. I was just at the grocery store, and I saw this poster. Looks like our competition is raising its ugly face."

"Hey, you haven't seen anything, girl. Those posters are plastered all over town. I hear they're even talking this up to the students, trying to get them to talk to their parents about it. Looks like they're out to win."

"So, what else can we do? Do you think we have a chance?"

Essie's stomach growled as the queasy feeling inside her developed at the thought of losing their fight.

"Don't you dare give up. The application has been sent. I took lots of pictures, and quite frankly, I believe we have an excellent chance of being approved."

"You'll let me know if there's anything I can do?"

"I will, but it looks like this is our only chance. I just hope they don't dilly-dally around until it's too late. Sometimes these things can take forever."

It was a busy time for Essie. She cleaned and dusted everything, searched through the closets, and found a white linen tablecloth, washed her nana's good china, and polished the silverware. School started back up, and the temperature warmed slightly. She planned her menu precisely, down to the time she'd put the turkey in and take it out of the oven. On the day before Thanksgiving, she baked her pies. Instead of the traditional pumpkin, she baked a sweet potato pie, always a favorite of hers, and of course, pecan.

Up early on Thanksgiving morning, she had her turkey in the oven by nine o'clock. Preparations were well underway with the rest of the dinner when everyone arrived. Mr. Winters, an older version of Lark, quickly made himself at home and was soon deep in discussion with Pete and Lark about the Green Bay Packers and Wisconsin Badgers. Mrs. Winters, a small, vivacious woman, joined Essie in the kitchen and insisted on helping.

"My dear, it's so sweet of you to have us here for dinner. Although it wasn't at all necessary," Mrs. Winters said.

Essie chuckled. "Maybe it was more necessary than you know. I ran across Lark buying a turkey. He was planning on cooking it himself."

Mrs. Winters slapped herself on the forehead. "Heaven

help us. Thank you, dear. You're an angel. And you have a beautiful home. I would love a tour later if you don't mind."

"Thank you. It was left to me by my nana. I would be glad to show you, but first, we should get this food on the table before it gets cold."

"I don't mean to be nosy, but may I ask how you met Lark? He tells me you haven't been in town long."

"Of course. Actually, I met him through Joey. Joey and my son are inseparable. It's a long story, but has Lark told you anything about how Jamie came to be here?"

"A short version. A sad story, but how wonderful for you." The older woman hesitated a moment. "Lark doesn't open up to everyone. He had a rough beginning, losing Jane. I don't think he could go through that again. The only thing that kept him going was Joey. That little boy is his whole life. Thank you for being his friend."

The overwhelming love that only a mother could have for her child came through in those words. Essie knew, in her own way, that Lark's mother was telling her to be gentle with her son's heart.

Dinner was a success. The turkey, golden brown, with stuffing and gravy, mashed potatoes, green bean casserole, *Jello* salad, candied yams, and Essie's own specialty, creamed carrots, got many compliments from everyone. Dessert was eaten later in the afternoon, after which Lark and his parents left, laden with leftovers.

Essie made herself a cup of tea, curled her feet underneath her, and settled back in the big, overstuffed chair. Inhaling deeply, she thought about all the things on her agenda.

December was always an exciting time of the year, and it would be Essie's first Christmas with Jamie. One of her biggest wishes was to make those same happy memories for Jamie that she had right here in this house. She could still see the sadness in his eyes at times when he sat alone, or when he saw or heard something that reminded him of Miss Ida. Essie became more determined than ever to erase those memories and replace them with happy ones. It was her duty and a promise to Miss Ida, and she intended to do her best to keep that promise.

When she got the call from Martha saying it wasn't official yet, but she was ninety-nine percent sure their application to the National Historical Registry was accepted, Essie suddenly felt a sad place in her heart for Lark. It wasn't easy to lose, especially something he felt so strongly about. For some time now, an idea had been banging around in her head. She made an appointment to discuss it with Martha.

Amidst all else that was going on, Essie got a call from Emma, her best friend from Tulsa, telling her she was coming for a visit. Although overwhelmed by her schedule, she would simply make time for Emma because she'd never needed her friend's listening ear more than she did now.

In a state of confusion about Lark and her suspicion of his keeping the truth about Diana from her, she lay awake many nights. She recalled the hours she and Emma spent in the past, hashing over their problems, listening to each other venting over boyfriends, and giggling over silly little things that young girls do. She missed this the most in her life since she came to Rosepoint.

Essie drove to Mt. Harmon airport and waited for the plane to land. When she saw Emma, she ran to her, and they jumped into each other's arms so vigorously that they almost fell.

"Girlfriend, do you know how much I've missed you?" Essie asked. She uncoiled her arms from around Emma and squeezed her face between her hands.

Essie couldn't take her eyes off her friend. Just as she remembered her, Emma's long dark hair hung loosely over her shoulders, enhanced by her sparkling brown eyes and a cute little nose that slightly tipped upward. It reminded Essie of a plant desperately aching for the sunlight, and she wondered if Emma turned often, her nose would grow the other way.

"I've missed you, too," Emma said. "And I can't believe you're a mama. I'm so excited to meet Jamie."

"Oh, Emma, I can't wait to tell you all about him. He's such a cute little dumpling and the most important thing in my life. I'm just scared to death. What do I know about being a mother?"

"What does anyone know in the beginning? You learn as you go. You'll be fine."

They stood near baggage claim waiting for Emma's suitcase. Essie was frowning. "But I let him almost break his arm. What kind of a mother is that?"

Emma looked at Essie and shook her head. "I see I have a lot of straightening out to do with that Brad-shy mind of yours. I swear, I never saw anyone who could drain the confidence out of a person like he could. Tell me, how many times did you break your arm when you were growing up?" Emma spotted her suitcase and grabbed it off the line.

Essie laughed. "Two times."

"Did that make your mom a bad parent?"

"No, my mom was the best. Did I tell you Brad called me?"

"Oh no, what did he want?" Emma asked.

"Nothing, just being sarcastic. I hung up on him."

When they drove up to Essie's house sometime later, Essie felt an unworthy sense of pride as Emma took in the scene before her. It was a stately-looking place, as Lark had labeled it. Along with all the repairs that had been done, the new paint job had given it a place of dignity among the neat row of Victorian homes stretched out along her street.

"Wow, I don't know if I'm worthy to enter your castle, your nobleness. Maybe you should drop this poor waif off at the back door."

Essie detected a note of awe when Emma spoke. The look of amazement on her face tickled Essie. "Quite a difference between this and that tiny apartment I had, huh?"

"I can see why you don't miss the city. It's beautiful." She stood and took in the scene before her.

Essie took Emma through the house, showing her friend all the improvements that she'd made. Afterward, she settled her in the guest room next to her own. Then they went downstairs, and Emma sat at the table while Essie made egg salad sandwiches and poured fresh lemonade for each of them.

"So, what time do I get to meet this little dumpling of yours?" Emma asked.

"Lark will drop him off after school. Usually around three-thirty." Essie set the sandwich down and handed Emma a glass of lemonade.

"Is his hair really as red as it looks in that picture you sent?"

"Every bit. You should have seen him at Halloween. I dressed him as a carrot." Essie giggled, remembering how cute he and Joey looked.

"I can tell you're very proud of him," Emma said.

"Oh, Emma, I can't tell you how much. He's the best thing that's ever happened to me."

"So, tell me about this handsome schoolteacher you say is always wanting you to go out with him." Emma flipped her dark hair back behind her shoulder. "Sounds like somebody you better hang on to."

Essie's heart missed a beat just thinking about Lark. "His name is Lark, and his son, Joey, is Jamie's best friend." She blushed. "He's so sweet and patient, but he's also involved with a lady teacher. Yes, he tells me he wants to get to know me better, but how can that be if he's still going out with her?" She took a big bite of her sandwich and gulped as she swallowed.

"Have you ever talked to him about it?"

"Not really. Don't you think he'd know that I wouldn't want him going out with someone else? I've seen them hugging and kissing." Essie fiddled with her glass, wiping the cool drops of condensation off as they trickled down the side of the glass.

"Does he know you know about her?" Emma asked.

"Of course. I've met her a couple of times. She's a nice lady."

"I think you should tell him it's either you or her. Fight for your man, girl. You let people run all over you." Emma got up and gave Essie a hug.

Was Emma right? Should she fight for Lark? Miss Ida had said the same thing to her, and so had Pete. But where did Diana stand in all this?

"If I can't have him all to myself, I won't get involved. Besides, there are other things going on that I haven't told you about." Essie shook her head. "I have a big enough job raising Jamie."

"Don't you use that for an excuse." Emma pointed her finger at Essie. "I know you. You need a man in your life, and so does Jamie."

"I do have a man in my life. He's my friend Pete, and he'd do anything for me. I've told you about him. He's done more around here than I have."

"It's not the same, and you know it. Or is there something going on between you two?" Emma looked uncertainly at Essie.

"No, definitely not. He's my friend, that's all. Besides, he told me he's a confirmed bachelor." Essie giggled. "He's such a character. Just wait until you meet him."

After their talk, they did the dishes, then Essie sat with Emma while she unpacked her clothes. All settled, the two bundled up and went outside. Essie showed Emma the boys' clubhouse, and they chatted about all the things going on in both their lives until it was time for Jamie to come home.

When Essie heard Lark's truck approaching, she stepped outside onto the porch and waved Lark and Joey inside. Jamie ran ahead and gave Essie a hug.

"Come on, Joey, let's go up and play in my fort," Jamie said. He turned to go as Essie caught him by the hand.

"Hold on, Jamie, we have company, and I want you to meet her. I want all of you to meet her." Essie motioned to Lark to come inside.

Emma, standing at the window watching, quickly stepped back and waited for them to enter.

Essie took Jamie by the hand and led him to Emma. "Emma, this is my son, Jamie. Say hello to Miss Emma, sweetheart."

"Hello," Jamie said shyly, hovering close to his mama.

Emma took his hand. "Hello, Jamie. It's so nice to meet you." She smiled down at him. "And this must be your buddy, Joey, I've been hearing so much about. Hi, Joey!"

Joey grinned. "Can we go play now?"

Jamie looked up at Essie. "Can we, Mama?"

"Sure, go ahead, and don't forget to change your clothes." The boys took off upstairs.

Emma laughed. "I see I really made an impression on them."

Lark chuckled. "Don't feel bad. When those two are together, they're in a world of their own." He walked over to Emma and offered his hand. "Hi, I'm Lark Winters, Joey's dad."

Essie watched closely as the two shook hands. Emma had always been her critic, and her opinion was important. At times, when Essie and Lark were together like this, she pretended he was her Lark. She was anxious to hear what Emma thought.

177

When Lark and Joey left a while later, Essie couldn't wait to hear what Emma had to say about Lark. "Well, what do you think?" she asked.

"I think Jamie's adorable," Emma answered.

Essie slapped Emma on the back. "Of course he's adorable, but you know what I mean."

Emma opened her purse, took two credit cards from her wallet, and plopped them down on the table. "I'm laying my cards on the table," she said. "If you don't go after that gorgeous man, I will. He's perfect, and anyone can see he's gaga over you."

"Do you really think so?" Essie asked earnestly.

"One look at those eyes, and there's no doubt about it. What's wrong with you, girlfriend? Go after that man with a vengeance."

"But what about Diana? I don't know what role she plays in this."

"The easiest way to find out is to ask him. It's my guess that he would give up half of paradise for you."

It didn't take long for Jamie to get over his shyness around Emma. They played games. They bundled up and went for walks together. Emma got down on the floor and crawled into Jamie's tent, or fort, as he called it. She even dressed up like a pilot and flew his make-believe airplane. Essie was delighted that her best friend had also become Jamie's friend.

When Pete dropped by that second evening after Emma came, Jamie was excited to introduce him to his new friend.

"Mr. Pete!" He ran to him and jumped up into his arms.

"Hey, buddy, how's my partner doing?" Pete asked.

"I'm good. I got a new friend. Well, she's really Mama's friend, but she's mine, too. Come on." He took Pete's hand and pulled him toward Essie, who stood watching.

Going over to Essie, Pete put his arm around her and gave

her a kiss on the cheek. "Sorry I'm late for dinner, honey. Hope you saved me some."

Essie laughed. "Get out of here, you freeloader." She gave him a playful shove, then took his hand and pulled him toward Emma. "Pete, this is my friend Emma from Tulsa."

Emma reached out her hand to him, but he shook his head. "Never let it be said that Pete shook the hand of a fair maiden. Wouldn't want to ruin my somewhat tarnished reputation." He pulled her to him in a big hug.

Essie looked at Emma, who was smiling. "Don't pay him no mind, Emma. He's harmless. Most of the time, we just ignore him."

"That's me. Ignored and neglected," Pete said.

"Poor baby," Essie said, patting him on the back.

"If you're not feeding me, I need to be going. I just stopped by to meet your friend." Pete pouted after an hour of his usual jesting.

After Pete left and Jamie was in bed, Essie and Emma sat in the parlor and talked. "You're so lucky to have such good friends," Emma said. "Pete's a riot. Where's he from, anyway? He sure doesn't talk much about himself."

"And he won't, either." Essie spread her hands and shrugged her shoulders. "Nobody knows where he's from. He gets really huffy if you ask him."

Emma looked at Essie in awe. "You're kidding. I wonder why."

Essie cleared her throat and hesitated a moment. "There's something I have to tell you about Pete. I don't want you to get upset because I don't believe it."

"Oh no, you're scaring me a little. You're not running around with someone dangerous, are you?"

"No, nothing like that. Some people think he might be dealing drugs, but I don't think that at all."

"What makes them think that?" Emma asked.

"For one thing, he doesn't work, and he always seems to have money. Then, there's this old, abandoned farm just down the road. Rumors are he's been seen there with a seedy-looking character." Essie raked her fingers through her hair. "In fact, I saw him there myself, and he was talking about some kind of deal. I've never told anyone about that."

Emma's mouth flew open, and she slapped her hand across her mouth. "Oh no," she gasped. "Do you remember that telephone call he got tonight?"

Essie nodded. "He's always on the phone. That doesn't mean anything."

"Yes, but when I came out of the bathroom, guess what I heard him say? It didn't mean anything to me at the time, but it just might now."

"Oh no! What did he say?" Essie's hopes dipped at the thought of something shady going on with Pete.

"He was saying something about, *Just call me when it's ready,* and, *We got to be careful and not let anybody see us.*"

Essie's sucked in her breath between her teeth, then slowly exhaled. She'd tried so hard not to believe the rumors about Pete, but as more and more little circumstances surfaced, it was hard to put them out of her mind. It wasn't like she was afraid of him, but it would break her heart if she knew he was involved in something illegal.

With the Christmas season coming up, Essie knew she'd be pressed for time, and she wanted to make the best of her friend's visit. "Would you like to go Christmas shopping with me?" Essie asked Emma one sunny afternoon. "I'm so anxious to get started, and you can help me pick out Jamie's presents."

"Oh, let's do it!" Emma clapped her hands together. "I want to buy him something cool, and this way, I won't have to mail it."

"And something else I've been thinking about . . . I want to get Jamie a puppy."

"A puppy!" Emma laughed. "You're not spoiling him very much, are you?"

Essie grinned. "I know, but every little boy should have a puppy. I remember the first dog I ever had was a present from Nana, right here in this house. I was five years old."

"Oh, you've never told me you had a dog before. What kind was it?"

"It was a beagle. There's nothing cuter than a little beagle puppy. I loved that little dog. His name was Rex."

"Aw, I wish I could be here. I love dogs, especially puppies. I'd like to see his face when he gets it."

Feeling caught up in the excitement of the moment, Essie spoke. "Let's do it after school today. We have an animal shelter right here in Rosepoint. That way, you'll be able to meet the whole family before you go back."

"Really, can we?" Emma grabbed Essie and hugged her. "Jamie will be so excited. Does he know he's getting one?"

"We've talked about it, but I told him later, maybe after the holidays."

"I bet you were excited when your nana gave you Rex. Did your parents know you were getting it?"

"I don't know, but I'm pretty sure Nana wouldn't have gotten him if she hadn't asked them first. She gave him to me at Christmas. They put him in a box, and when Daddy brought the box out, I could see the lid bouncing up and down. It scared me so bad I ran to Nana. I wouldn't go near the box. Daddy finally took him out and gave him to me."

"Why were you scared?

"I was five years old. Who knows? A lot of those robot toys were popular, and I was scared to death of them. I must have thought it was a monster or something. I don't want to scare him. I just want it to be fun for him."

"Maybe you could just have it running around here when

he gets home from school."

"No, I'd like him to pick out the one he wants. I guess I'll just have to tell him." Essie jumped up and grabbed Emma's hand. "Come on! I'm so excited I can't just sit here. Let's go bake some cookies or something. One of the fondest memories I have is making cut-out cookies with Nana at Christmas. She had so many cookie cutters and all that glitter. I remember we used to put glitter on each other's noses and dance around like silly fairies. I called her Nana Glitter-nosed. And I'd go with her while she took them around the neighborhood and gave most of them away. I can't wait to do that with my son." Love radiated from her heart, both for Jamie and her nana.

The two friends had their cookies made and cooling when Jamie got home from school. Lark came in with Joey following close behind.

"I thought maybe your friend would like to try some of our famous pizza from Uncle Ziggy's," Lark said. "I'd like to take you there if you don't have other plans." Lark put his hands in his pockets and patiently waited for Essie to answer.

Essie looked at Emma. "We do have plans, but I think we can fit it in somehow. Little Pizza Queen over there would never forgive me if we turned down an offer like that." She nodded toward Emma. "Let me give the boys a snack, and I'll fill you in."

Essie poured milk for Jamie and Joey and sat them at the kitchen table with cookies. They went into the parlor, and she spoke softly to Lark. "We're going to the animal shelter to get a puppy for Jamie. He doesn't know yet, but you and Joey can come, too. Joey can help him pick it out." She put her hand to her mouth. "Oh, I hope that won't be a problem with Joey."

"Not at all. We've had this discussion before. He knows there's no one home all day to take care of a puppy." Lark chuckled. "Besides, he's over here just about as much as he's at home. He'll be thrilled."

"Good, then you'll go with us?" Essie asked. "We can go for pizza afterwards. If we find a dog he likes, hopefully, they'll hold it for us until tomorrow. I'll have to get a kennel and all kinds of supplies. Emma and I are going to Mt. Harmon shopping anyway."

Lark looked at her and rolled his eyes. "If he can find one he likes! Are you kidding? They'll both want everyone they see."

"Sounds like a plan. Let's go tell them." They all headed for the kitchen where the boys were just finishing their snack.

"Who likes surprises?" Essie hollered as they entered the kitchen.

"I do!" Both boys jumped up and clapped their hands.

Lark winked at Essie. "We're all going for pizza. How's that for a surprise?"

"Yeah!" The boys held hands and danced around in a circle.

"But first, I think this house needs a little puppy really bad, don't you, Jamie?" Essie asked. "One that can snuggle with you at night and keep you warm in the bed."

The look of dazzlement on Jamie's face was precious. When he finally realized what Essie was saying, he ran to her and threw his arms around her. "Do you mean it, Mama? Can I really get a puppy?"

"Yes, if we can find one you want." Essie's heart delighted at the joy she saw on Jamie's face.

"I can find one. I'll find the bestest one in the whole wide world. When can we go? Joey, you and me can find him the bestest name, and you can come play with him all the time. He'll be like both of our buddies. Can we go now? Please, Mama," Jamie begged.

They were all laughing. "We can go now, but you have to listen to me." Essie grabbed Jamie gently by the arms and stood holding him until he settled down. "We don't know how many they have there now, so maybe you won't find the one you want today, but if we do find one, you can't bring it home with you tonight."

She watched as disappointment clouded Jamie's face. "We'll need a collar and a leash, and he'll need a kennel and special food to eat and a lot of other things, but if we do find one, we can bring him home tomorrow."

Jamie brightened up. "Promise?"

"I promise."

As they left for the shelter, the boys went with Lark in his truck. He led the way, and as Essie drove up to the animal shelter, the boys were already running into the big sprawling building.

Following them in, Essie and Emma passed a small waiting room with chairs arranged around a table piled high with old magazines with curly edges. Essie made a mental note to drop off some more recent ones. They were greeted with a melodious harmony of barking, yipping, and baying, providing a tuneful welcome to the guests coming in through the wide door that led to a row of double-stacked kennels on each side.

Lark took each of the boys by the hand as they walked down the wide aisle that separated the two stacks of kennels. They stopped in front of each kennel that was occupied, talking to the large variety of dogs and petting the ones the attendant gave them permission to.

In the last kennel, away from the others, were three small puppies sleeping peacefully, their tiny little bellies rising and falling with each breath they took. Cuddling together, one puppy's head was thrown limply over the other's neck, and they looked like three little bean bags piled together just waiting for someone to toss them.

"Aw," they all murmured as they gathered in front of the kennel.

"What kind are they?" Essie asked the attendant.

"All American mutts." The friendly attendant laughed. "I believe they have some beagle in them."

"Then they won't get too big?"

"I'm guessing they won't. Of course you never know." The attendant reached inside the cage, picked up two of the puppies, and handed them to the boys. He handed the other one to Essie. The little puppies wagged their tails and licked the boys' faces. They were mostly black, with brown ears, and a few white spots scattered across their noses. Only one of them had four white feet.

As the puppies wiggled and squirmed, the boys passed them around so everyone could get a chance to hold them. Essie could see it would be a hard decision for Jamie to make.

"So what do you think?" she asked. "And no, you can't have them all." She laughed and squeezed Jamie to her.

"I feel so bad for the ones that have to stay here in that cage."

The attendant winked at Essie. "They won't be here long. Two other people are coming tomorrow. So you just get the first pick, that's all."

"You'll have to pick, bud," Lark said.

Jamie looked at Emma. "Which one do you like?"

Emma was quick to answer. "I like the one with the white boots."

Joey jumped up and down and clapped his hands. "Me, too. I was hoping you'd pick him."

"Me, too. I think I like him best," Jamie finally declared.

Essie gave a sigh of relief. She whispered to Lark and Emma. "I was afraid he'd choose the female. We don't need a house full of puppies."

Essie took care of all the details of the adoption and decided to pick the puppy up the next afternoon.

When they got to Ziggy's, Lark draped his arm loosely over

Essie's shoulder as they entered. She was happy, and this was one of those moments she felt like he was her Lark. Then, she recalled seeing him kissing Diana, and the old doubts returned.

Jamie and Joey were busy trying to find a name for his puppy. "I want my puppy to have the neatest name in the world," Jamie said to Joey.

"Yeah, not like Spot or Fido. Everybody names their dogs that."

"What about Pushkin, like our play?" Jamie pondered.

Joey shook his head. "Yeah, but that's a pug name. Your puppy's not a pug."

Emma watched the two little boys struggling to find a name. "If it was my puppy, I know what I would call him. I would call him Boots. Remember his feet? He has four white boots on."

Jamie's eyes popped open wide in excitement. "That's the goodest name yet. I'll call him Mr. Boots, and everybody will inspect him 'cause he's a Mr."

Essie laughed. "I think you mean respect."

"Yeah, I can't wait for tomorrow when I can bring Mr. Boots home."

They ate their pizza amid chatter about Mr. Boots. They all thanked Lark and drove home, anxiously awaiting the new addition to their family.

Lark paid the bill and watched as they left. Tonight was one of those nights he let his imagination pretend Essie was all his. He loved the family atmosphere with Essie sitting beside him, and the two happy little boys, and even Essie and Emma chatting about old times. Why did Essie feel so reluctant to accept help when it came to Jamie? And why did she feel there was no room for anyone else in her life? He wasn't trying to take any of this away from her. He only wanted to share it with her.

"Boy, you can just see the want dripping off that guy, Essie," Emma said from the passenger seat. "And you can see it in your eyes every time you look at him. I'd be on that guy like a swarm of bees. I think you're coo-coo if you don't give him a chance."

After they all settled into bed later that night, Essie thought back on what Emma had said. She didn't deny that she was in love with Lark. And he certainly seemed to be interested in her. So what was keeping them apart? Was Miss Ida's house really an issue. Wasn't everyone entitled to their own opinion? There was only one issue, and it was Diana. Her mother had always told her, *Three is a crowd*. In her perfect dream, there was no room for another woman, and she would never be willing to compromise.

CHAPTER TWELVE

Joey begged his dad every day when they brought Jamie home from school to let him stay so he could help Jamie train Mr. Boots. The persistence that he and Jamie put into teaching Mr. Boots to do his job on the puppy pad in no way lessened the appearance of tiny wet spots throughout the house. Essie put together a bottle of cleaner and showed Jamie how to get rid of the spots. She marveled at his patience as she watched him squirt the liquid on the mess, take the small brush, and scrub.

Essie, wanting everything clean and in place, had agreed to have the meeting at her house that night. She and Martha decided it may help their cause by having on-site proof of what the restoration of an old Victorian home could be. Her cookies were baked, and freshly squeezed lemonade was made, along with all the makings of coffee in the big coffee urn she found in the basement. Joey begged to spend the night with Jamie, and they were upstairs in their pajamas with instructions to keep Mr. Boots occupied.

As the people began to come, excitement ran high. Determining the use of Miss Ida's house had been a hard-fought battle, and tonight it would be decided. No doubt, disappointment would come for some. Essie sat nervously, twiddling her thumbs, waiting for the meeting to begin. Glancing at Lark talking with Pete and the mayor, she wondered what their feelings toward each other would be like after tonight.

The mayor spoke briefly. "First, I would like to thank Essie for allowing us to meet in her beautiful home. You all know what our business agenda is tonight, so I'm not going to waste time. I'll turn the meeting over to Lark."

"Thank you, Mr. Mayor," he said, standing in the center of the room. "I'm glad to see we're all still on speaking terms." When the laughter died down, he continued. "We all knew Miss Ida, and I think we all agree that she'd welcome a little friendly competition. The only way I can think of doing this is to ask for a showing of hands, so all who are for using it for a badly needed rec center, raise your hand."

Essie watched as hands flew up all around the room. Suddenly Martha stood and spoke loudly. "I think I can save some time, Mr. Mayor, if I may have the floor for a moment."

He handed her the microphone. She waved a sheet of paper in the air. "I have in my hand a letter from the National Historical Registry that states in a very short time, Miss Ida's house will be registered as a historical property. Therefore, forbidding any changes to the structure." She stopped and looked over the very quiet audience. "But I do think Essie has something to say that will make you think this might be in the best interest of the residents of Rosepoint."

Essie held her breath, hoping her heartbeat couldn't be heard. She'd been dreading this moment, but also looking forward to it. She looked at Lark, sitting opposite her in the back row. And imagined she saw the color drain from his face. She stood to take the microphone, and when she glanced again, Lark was gone. Rattled, she pulled herself together, took the mic from Martha, and cleared her throat.

"I do hope what I have to say will send everyone home tonight with a smile on their face. As you know, Mr. Simmons has shut down the use of our very important community hall. Well, Martha and I have been negotiating with him for a while, trying to come to terms. I'm so happy to tell you that I just found out shortly before this meeting that Mr. Simmons has agreed to sell the hall back to me for the same amount of money my grandfather sold it to him for. I'll be donating it to the city in honor of my grandparents. And, with it sitting empty except for special occasions, won't it make an excellent rec center?" She paused, watching the reaction of the crowd. Among whoops and hollers, the audience broke into applause. She held up her hand to quiet them. "To start things rolling, I'm donating five hundred dollars to start a fund for supplies and furnishings. Martha oversees any donations that I know you're going to give generously. Now, let's have some refreshments."

Essie couldn't keep the smile off her face, but her only disappointment was the absence of Lark. Ever since she got the final word from Matt Simmons, she'd imagined what he would do.

Lark couldn't believe he'd slipped out Essie's back door. He found himself walking in the brisk, fresh air without his jacket. As he listened to Martha's words, the dreams he'd worked for these last weeks vanished. He drew in a big gasp of cold air and watched the smoke as he exhaled. The idea of the historical thing never crossed his mind in all these weeks, so he wondered why Essie didn't discuss it with him. In all fairness, he probably would have done the same thing. He felt the shivers run through his whole body. It was freezing out. He turned and walked rapidly back to his truck, got in, and drove toward home. He realized walking out was rude, but right now, he couldn't face the crowd. For the first time in years, he'd given no thought to Joey, not even saying goodnight, so as guilt hit him, he knew he'd go back.

Essie's house echoed with laughter and happy sounds. Their problem, which they gathered tonight to solve, concluded itself into the perfect solution. Plans and ideas floated from one group to another, some digging deep into their pockets to donate to the new fund. Essie drew a big breath as the last of the stragglers thanked her and left.

She hurried upstairs and settled the boys into bed. While bracing herself to confront the pile of dirty cups and glasses, she jumped when she heard the doorbell. Perhaps someone was looking for a scarf or gloves left behind. She hurried to the door, and her mouth flew open when she saw Lark standing there.

Opening the door, she stepped back for him to enter. She could see the desperation in his eyes.

"Am I too late to say goodnight to Joey?" He hesitated for a moment. "I'm sorry, Essie, I sort of lost it there for a minute. I-I just . . ."

She laid her hand on his shoulder. "It's okay. You go up and say goodnight to Joey. I just put them to bed. Come back down, and we'll talk."

She watched him climb the stairs, then began to collect the cups and glasses and carried them into the kitchen, a little nervous, yet very excited to tell him the good news. She put together a plate of cookies and poured two glasses of lemonade, and set them at the table. When she heard Jamie's door close, she met him at the bottom of the stairs.

She grabbed him by the hand and led him to the table. "You missed out on refreshments. I know how much you love cookies." The compassion she felt for him at this moment was overwhelming, and she couldn't wait to put a smile on his face.

He gave her a half-hearted smile, chose a cookie from the plate, and took a drink of lemonade. "Like I said, I'm so sorry, Essie, but have you ever lost a dream? I want you to know, it's nothing against you. You won fair and square."

She could see those beautiful eyes begging for her to

understand. "Lark, you missed the most important part of the meeting." She grinned, a feeling of elation overtaking her emotions. "I'm buying back the community hall and donating it to Rosepoint. Don't you see, it stands empty most of the time, and it'll be perfect for a rec center for the youth. We've already started a fund for equipment and furnishings, and can you believe it, we have over two thousand dollars already. The residents are too excited about it." She giggled.

Lark's whole body jerked to attention. His eyes sparkled as he reached across the table and grabbed her hand. "You aren't kidding me, are you? That's perfect. It's even better than Miss Ida's house. Now we can have both projects, but how did it happen? How did you persuade Matt to sell the hall back to you?" He squeezed her hands.

"Martha and I worked our magic. Besides, he wasn't about to let the hall sit there and rot, not when he could get his money back." She pulled her hands free. "I'd better get this mess cleaned up. I don't care to face a sink full of dirty dishes in the morning."

He got up and came around the table and caught her on each arm. "I'll help you, but first, I have some urgent business to attend to." He grinned at her, his eyes shining. He hugged her tightly and pushed her back down to the chair. Pulling another chair up beside her, he again grabbed both her hands in his.

Essie's heart was racing a mile a minute. The feel of his hands on hers sent goose bumps up her spine as she waited with anticipation.

His eyes stared steadily into hers as he spoke. "Essie, you must know I'm crazy about you. I can't think about anything else, and I think you have feelings for me, too. That's why I can't understand why you won't go out with me. Will you let me in on the secret?"

Essie could feel herself tense, and she knew Lark could feel it, too. Was it time to discuss Diana with him? Pete and Emma both thought so. She took a deep breath and let it out slowly. "Lark, there's the problem of Diana. The three of us is too many. I'm sorry, but I just can't share you with another woman."

He pressed his lips together tight and shook his head. "Just as I thought." Hesitating a moment, he never let her eyes go. "Essie, Diana and my relationship is strictly platonic. She's a friend, and I'm helping her out, that's all."

Essie tried hard to believe him, but she couldn't erase that image of them wrapped in each other's arms and kissing passionately. He wasn't telling her the whole truth, and she wasn't ready to willingly accept what he told her.

She drew in a big breath. "I'm sorry, Lark, but I think it's best if we're just friends." She could see the disappointment in his eyes, and her heart hurt more than she thought possible as he let go of her hands and stood.

"We'd better get those dishes washed. Come on." He held out his hand. "I'll help you."

"On second thought," she said, ignoring his hand. "I'm tired. I'll do them in the morning."

"You sure? I'll be glad to help."

Essie shook her head, afraid if she spoke, her emotions would explode.

"Then I'll be going." He rose to his feet and started toward the door, suddenly stopping and turning to her. "By the way, congratulations. You're the town hero now. This town owes you a lot."

"It was my grandpa's money. It's what he would've wanted."

He paused for a moment, gazing at her, then turned to go.

She stood at the door and watched as he walked to his truck.

Essie felt so much love for Lark that the moment he left, her eyes filled with the tears she'd been able to control while he was still there. She went upstairs and listened at the boys' door. All was quiet, so she went to her bedroom and changed into her pajamas. Reasoning with herself, she knew she'd done the right thing, but she also knew sleep would be hard to come tonight.

Lark hurried to his truck, fumbled in his pocket for his keys, and wiped the moisture from his eyes as he placed the key into the ignition. It'd been a momentous night for Rosepoint, getting its hall back and gaining a much-needed rec center for the youth. His long-time dream was now a reality, yet his heart ached as he realized his situation. He wondered, had he broken his promise to Diana in an effort to secure Essie's love? Even then, he knew she didn't completely believe him, yet a part of him felt Essie was overwhelmed with the responsibility of raising Jamie. Why couldn't she understand she could accept help without breaking her promise to Miss Ida? He started his engine and drove off, feeling like he was losing Essie and like he'd betrayed Diana.

In the next few days, Essie kept herself busy decorating the house for the holidays. Today they were waiting for Pete to pick them up to go get their Christmas tree. Jamie, in his snow pants, pranced around the room, jumping with excitement, and Mr. Boots was jumping right along with him. Essie sighed with relief when she heard the doorbell.

On the ride to the farm, Essie told Jamie about how each Christmas her family would cut their own tree and take it home to decorate. They would all sit together around a roaring fire in the fireplace and string popcorn. Then Nana would get out her boxes of special ornaments, some of which Essie had made over the years. Essie could almost smell the fresh scent of pine as she told Jamie about how each year it was a tradition that her daddy would lift her up high on his shoulders so she could place the angel on the very top of the tree.

When they got to the tree farm, Essie laughed at Jamie. He was so bundled up that he could hardly walk. Pete took his saw and a large sled provided by the farm to get the tree back to their vehicle. He sat Jamie in the middle of the sled, and they took off down the well-beaten path through the trees. Jamie giggled as Pete exaggerated the movements of the sled to tip him from side to side.

When they got into the center of the growth, Essie told Jamie to start looking for their perfect tree. The first one Jamie pointed to was too fat.

"We need a big, tall one," she reminded him.

When Jamie pointed to another rather lopsided one, Pete made a snowball and tossed it gently at him.

"You're undoubtedly the worst Christmas tree picker-outter I have ever seen," Pete declared.

Jamie fell over, giggling. "I want that one," he said, as they slid by a *Charlie Brown* sapling.

By the time they located their perfect tree, it was getting a little dark, and the air was getting nippy.

"The first thing I'm going to do when we get home is make hot chocolate," Essie said.

"The first thing I'm doing is giving Mr. Boots a hug." Jamie stuck his bottom lip out in a big pout. "He wanted to come with us, but Mama wouldn't let him."

"We should have brought him. I bet he could have picked out a better tree than you," Pete teased. "You had better get that lip tucked back in, or I'm going for another snowball." He scooped up a handful of snow.

Jamie slumped down and covered his face, giggling. "No, no!" he hollered.

By the time they got home and got the tree unloaded, darkness had snuck upon them and they were all cold and tired. After warming up with a good cup of hot chocolate topped with creamy marshmallows, Pete put the tree in the stand and placed it in front of the big bay window in the parlor, looking out toward the street.

Essie popped a pan of popcorn and showed Jamie how to string the fluffy corn into a row, warning him to be careful of the blunt needle she found in Nana's knitting bag.

Tempted by the dangling string of fluffy white kernels dancing around before him, Mr. Boots pounced on Jamie's string and nibbled at the treat.

"Mama," Jamie hollered. "Mr. Boots is eating my decorations." He dove for the rambunctious little puppy and enfolded him in his arms. "Naughty boy," he scolded.

"Maybe you should share a few of those you've been sneaking into your mouth," Pete said, reaching over and patting the puppy's fat little belly.

Jamie grinned. "I can't help it. Mama makes such good popcorn."

"I think we have enough popcorn for Santa and all his elves, so who wants to hang some ornaments?" Essie asked, examining the strings they had finished.

"I do! I do!" Jamie danced around with Mr. Boots jumping at his heels.

"Me, too." Pete jumped up and pulled Essie into a dance circle with Jamie. "Why don't I put the lights on while you two get the ornaments?" he suggested.

In the chaos of loading the tree with ornaments, beads, tinsel, and candy canes, Mr. Boots wound up rolling around with a small bulb he'd swiped off the bottom branch of the tree. He batted at it with his paw, pushed it across the floor with his nose, and chewed the tassel that was attached.

"Mr. Boots," Jamie and Essie echoed. Jamie fell to the floor, wrestling the bulb away from the puppy, and was immediately attacked with licks and kisses from the happy little creature. They rolled on the floor together while Essie relocated the lower ornaments to higher branches.

"I guess we'll have to put a fence around our tree, or he'll have all the presents unwrapped by Christmas time." Essie reached over and ruffled the hair on Mr. Boot's back. "You little pest."

Jamie grabbed the puppy and hugged him. "He's not a pest, Mama. He just don't know any better, do you, Mr. Boots?"

Pete climbed the step ladder with Jamie in front of him and held on to the boy while Jamie settled the old-time angel on top. The angel was dressed in white, trimmed with gold, with long blonde curls flowing generously over her wings. The angel had been on Nana's tree every year, as far back as Essie could remember.

As Essie stepped back and watched the two placing the angel on the tree, it completed that certain picture that brought forth a flood of memories of her Christmases with Nana.

"Ta-da!" Pete stretched his hand toward the tree. "Are you ready for the lights?" he asked.

"Yeah!" Jamie jumped up and down.

When Pete plugged the lights in, they all stood in awe, staring at the huge tree, so magnificently adorned in all its splendor, spreading its welcome to all who entered the front door.

Essie took a small box from the table and opened it. She pulled out a little heart ornament with a red ribbon tied through a tiny hole in the top. As she held it in the palm of her hand, lovingly stroking it, it was obvious it was precious to her.

"This ornament has a special place on the tree, and it's always the last one to go on each year. Sit down, and I'll tell you about it."

Jamie and Pete sat, and she held the ornament out for them to see. The little hardwood heart, roughly carved, had writing scratched into the back.

"Years ago, when Nana and Grandpa were first married, times were hard, and there weren't many jobs to be found. Grandpa took a job in a logging camp, and he didn't get to come home very often. He had no car, and the only way he could get to see his new bride was to walk. About a month into his job, he was determined to make it home to see her. He started out with two other men, and it was raining hard. When they got to the point where they couldn't go any further, they found lodging in an old hunting cabin. Tired and cold, they built a fire in the wood stove, and the two other men went to bed. But Grandpa was determined to take his beloved something to show her how much he'd missed her. Even though he was worn out from walking all day, he found a piece of wood somewhere and stayed up all night whittling this heart for her." She turned it over and rubbed her hand across the writing. "He wrote, I will love you forever."

She looked at Pete and saw a tear roll down his cheek. She reached over and touched him. "Don't tell me our tough Mr. Pete is crying," she said.

"Just got something in my eye." He chuckled as he rubbed his hand across his face. "That's so sweet! Can I ask you a big favor? Can I help you hang it?"

"Of course! Come on, Jamie, you can help, too." They all took the ribbon and placed the little wooden ornament in its special place on the tree.

When Lark dropped Jamie off after school on Monday, Jamie brought them in to see their tree.

"And Mama said we might have to put a fence around it 'cause Mr. Boots will tear open all our presents." The boys were on the floor, rolling, with Mr. Boots viciously slinging his new knotted rope toy from side to side. "Is your tree as big as ours?" Jamie asked Joey.

"We don't have ours yet."

"You don't have yours yet? Oh boy!" He slapped himself on the head. "You better hurry up. Christmas is only three weeks away."

Essie and Lark, listening to the conversation, laughed.

"It's not one of my most talented sides," Lark admitted. "I have an artificial tree in the basement. It doesn't take much time to drag it up the stairs and throw a few things on it."

Essie looked at him in astonishment. "Lark Winters! Wipe out that mouth of yours. How can you be serious?" She looked forward to Christmas more than anything else, and to think of Lark and Joey without a proper tree made her sad. "I'll be glad to come help you decorate. Just let me know when it's a good time for you."

"Mrs. Jordan is coming to help like she always does, remember, Daddy? She even said we should throw away that old, ragged tree we have and go cut one." Joey rolled his eyes. "You're always telling me I forget everything. She just told you that when she came over and cooked us dinner the other night."

Lark looked uncomfortable. He shifted his eyes away from Essie. "Yes, I guess I did forget."

"Well, good for her," Essie said. "I'm sure you'll have a beautiful tree." She kept her eyes from meeting Lark's.

As Lark and Joey left, Essie was more convinced than ever that she had made the right decision about her future.

Essie, busy baking cookies the next day, got a call from Rob Sheffield. "I have some good news for you," he told her. "I talked to the judge today, and he said the final adoption papers are ready. Since there's no objection to Miss Ida's wishes, it's just a matter of meeting with him and signing your name a couple of times. Then Jamie is legally your son. Nobody can take him away from you. Congratulations!"

Essie was so elated she lost all control. The cup of flour she had in her hand flew into the air and landed directly on Mr. Boots. She picked him up, dusted him off, and danced around the kitchen with him. Looking upward with a grateful heart, she said, "Thank you! Thank You!"

She ran for her phone and called Pete. Not even bothering to say hello when he answered, she hollered into the phone, "He's mine! He's mine! Jamie's all mine!"

Pete was laughing. "Calm down, girl, before you burst a lung. I take it the adoption papers came through."

"Yes! Yes! Yes! Oh, thank you God." She was breathless, her mind racing with excitement. "You have to come over. We have to have a party for him. Chicken. He loves fried chicken. That's what I'll make. You'll come over, won't you?"

"I wouldn't miss it for anything. I'll be there shortly."

When Lark dropped Jamie off after school, Essie and Pete were waiting anxiously. Her final decision to not involve Lark in her personal affairs anymore and to distance herself from him as much as possible had made it much easier when he drove away.

Jamie was always excited to see Mr. Pete. And, of course, Mr. Boots had been cleaned up, and the chicken was cooked and waiting. Essie grabbed Jamie and hugged him, picking him up and swinging him around. The uncertain smile on Jamie's lips brought Essie to the realization that Jamie didn't know what was going on.

Setting him down before her, Essie said to him, "Do you remember when we adopted Mr. Boots and I told you that made him an official member of this family?"

Jamie nodded his head. "You said nobody could ever take

him away from us."

"That's right, and today I just got word that your adoption is official. That means no one can ever take you away from me."

Jamie put his head on Essie's shoulder. "Me and Mr. Boots are both 'dopted. Does that mean we're brothers?" He giggled.

"I guess it does. I have two 'dopted boys, and no one can ever take either one of you away from me."

She tickled him, and Jamie ran over to Pete, yelling, "Save me!"

"And now we're going to celebrate by having an adoption party. How does that sound?"

"Can Mr. Boots celebrate 'cause he was 'dopted, too?"

"He sure can. Go change your clothes. I've made your favorite fried chicken for you, and Mr. Pete is staying to help us celebrate."

Caught up in the excitement, Jamie suddenly stopped and tugged at Essie's hand. "We could invite Joey and his daddy. They could help us celebrate."

Not wanting to disappoint him, Essie quickly thought of a way to explain to Jamie. "This is a very special family party just for you and me and Mr. Boots."

He looked toward the kitchen where Pete was setting the table. "But what about Mr. Pete? He's not part of our family."

She leaned close and whispered into his ear, "I know, but since he's already here, it wouldn't be nice to ask him to leave." She squeezed him hard. "Go change. We're almost ready."

They had just finished eating, and Essie and Pete were putting everything away when they heard the siren. The fire truck buzzed by in front of the house as they all three ran outside. Looking in the direction of the Sawyer place, they saw a small swirl of smoke.

The change that came over Pete shocked Essie. She watched as the color drained from his face.

He slapped himself on the cheek and ran for his truck. "Oh no! You stay here. I have to go."

"Be careful," Essie hollered, watching as he sped toward the scene.

Why was he so upset? No lives were in danger. In fact, considering all the things that had been going on there, maybe it was a good thing if it did burn. It was just an old, abandoned house. There was nothing of value there. Or was there? She remembered *the deal* she'd heard Pete discussing, and what about what Emma had heard? Could he have something hidden there?

She thought of her own house and all the memories it held. How heartbreaking it would be to see them go up in flames. What would it be like for the Sawyer family? Thinking back on the story Sam Howard had told her that day at the grocery store, she thought about the grandson, longing for his dad's attention and spending his happiest days at the Sawyer farm with his grandparents. Almost as if someone was whispering to her, a thought came to her. Could it be that Pete was that grandson? Was that why he was so upset?

"Mama, can we go see the fire?" Jamie asked.

"No, sweetheart, you heard Mr. Pete. He said to stay here. If a whole bunch of people showed up, they would just get in the way, and the firemen couldn't do their jobs."

"But why is Mr. Pete going? What if he gets in the way?"

"That's a good question. I really wish I knew," she said, more to herself than to Jamie.

It was late evening when Pete came back, and Essie noticed several dark smudges on his face and hands. His clothes were tousled and dirty. He looked exhausted, and his unusually quiet demeanor told her he was troubled.

"Tell me what happened. How much damage did it do?"

she asked worriedly.

"Not as bad as it could have been."

"Does anyone know how it started?"

"The chief figures it must have been some kids fooling around, and they started a fire in the fireplace to keep warm. The old chimney was probably clogged. The smoke had to go somewhere," Pete said gruffly.

"So there was never really a fire? It was just smoke?" Essie asked.

"Right. Someone passing by saw the smoke and called it in. Luckily one of the windows was broken, and the smoke was pouring out through that. Otherwise, the whole thing might have gone up."

"Someone should do something to keep those kids out of there. Where are the Sawyers? Why aren't they doing something?" Trying to read his reactions, Essie looked him straight in the eyes.

Pete shook his head. "Sorry I left in such a hurry. I . . . I just don't like fires. They make me nervous, especially when they're so close."

Two days later, Essie hadn't been able to put the fire and Pete's reaction to it out of her mind. But she came suddenly back to the present at the sound of Lark's truck. Despite her determination to put those feelings behind her, her heart gave that old familiar twitch.

From the kitchen, she heard the door open and the sounds of little feet trampling into the entryway. It wasn't unusual for Joey to be with Jamie, especially since Mr. Boots had become a part of their family. She set down the magazine she'd been reading and went to greet them, surprised to find Lark at the door, too.

"Is it okay if I come in for a minute?" Lark asked.

"Of course. Come on in." She stood back, somewhat

baffled at why he was there.

"Hi, Mama," Jamie said as he and Joey ran up the stairs, giggling.

Essie looked after Jamie. "Don't I even get a hug? He must have missed me terribly." She walked into the parlor with Lark following her.

"When those two little rugrats are together, don't be surprised at anything," Lark said, looking up the stairway.

Essie nodded in agreement. "So, Joey said your mom and dad were in town again. Did you have a good visit?"

"Yes, they left yesterday. Mom spent most of the time in the kitchen. She made up enough dinners to last us all the way through New Year's," Lark said with a laugh.

"She's a sweetheart. Just looking after her two boys."

"She's afraid Joey and I will starve. Not a chance. I always keep an extra jar of peanut butter and jelly." He grinned.

Hearing the muffled sound of laughter coming from the stairway, Essie turned to see two little spying heads as they quickly withdrew from sight. Remembering their conversation that she'd overheard the night she listened at the door, she smiled as she walked out of view and beckoned Lark to sit.

"Essie," Lark said.

Nervous at the way Lark's voice cracked as he said her name, she nodded for him to continue.

"You must know how I feel about you."

She could feel the tenderness in his hands as he reached for hers. Her heart raced as their eyes connected.

"I'm so in love with you." His eyes held hers as he stood completely still, waiting for her to say something.

She gasped softly, and with her eyes never leaving his, she spoke. "Lark, we talked about this. I think things are better left the way they are. I made a promise to Miss Ida. I have an obligation to Jamie." She looked away.

"I have enough room in my heart for Jamie. I was hoping you have room in your heart for me and Joey? Promise me you'll at least think about it."

"I will." She nodded her head. If only he knew how much she wanted to accept his love. Her burning desire to pull him to her and lose herself in his kiss, still couldn't overcome that stubborn part of her that demanded one hundred percent of him.

Lark dropped her hands and gently laid one palm against her cheek.

"Joey," he hollered up the stairs. "It's time to go, bud."

Sitting alone quietly after Jamie was tucked into bed, Essie found herself reflecting on Lark's words. "I'm so in love with you." She felt a tear drop as it trickled down her cheek. There was no doubt in her mind that she was in love with him. Yet there was that stubborn part of her that could never accept another woman being part of her relationship with Lark.

As she drove Jamie to school the next morning, she saw something that furthered her decision to distance herself from Lark. There they were, Diana and Lark, embracing in front of Diana's apartment building. With Essie's heart at its lowest point, she knew at that moment that it was all over for her and Lark. She would never accept a relationship that was not given wholeheartedly. Essie drove by, hoping they didn't see her.

To keep her mind occupied, Essie decided to clear out the last of her nana's personal things. The one dresser drawer she'd avoided until now held the story of Nana's last days. Her makeup, a comb, a half-empty bottle of her favorite perfume, and various bottles of pain medicine.

As she gathered the bottles to discard, she saw the edge of a small photo. Picking it up and looking it over closely, she gasped loudly, holding her mouth agape while her mind adjusted to the picture she held. In the photo was her nana and . . . Pete? No, it couldn't be! Maybe someone who looked like him. She looked closer. It was definitely Pete. But how could that be? He'd told her he'd only been in Rosepoint a year and a half and that he didn't know her nana. Her nana had been gone two years.

Pete had a lot of explaining to do. She turned the photo over, and what she saw there almost made her fall. She groped for the bed and sat down. Her heart pounded so hard she thought her chest would burst. Written in her nana's familiar handwriting was *Me and Tory.*

The only Tory she knew was her brother, and he was dead. She tried to recall what her parents had told her about him. They never would discuss the circumstances of his death. All they ever told her was that he was gone. As a three-year-old, that explanation was enough.

She had to get her wits about her. With trembling hands, she picked up her phone and called Pete, or Tory, or whoever he was.

"You need to get over here. I have to talk to you." She had no control over the tone of her voice.

"You sound upset. Are you all right?" Pete asked.

"Just come." She clicked her phone off. She knew he would be there within three minutes.

Pete burst into the room without knocking. Essie looked up, eyes searching Pete's face for an answer. One look at her, and he sat beside her.

"Okay, tell me what's going on."

The only other time she'd seen that look of panic on his face was when he saw the fire at the Sawyer farm.

Essie plopped the photo down in front of him. "No, you tell me what's going on." She watched him as the color drained from his face. She waited. "Are you my brother?" She'd never seen him without words.

He got up and walked to the window, shook his head and spread his hands nervously.

"You are, aren't you? But why didn't you tell me?" She clamped her jaw together and sucked in her breath. "*Oh,* I am so mad at you I could slap you right now." She looked at him with tears streaming down her face. "Come here." She held out her arms to him, and he walked into them.

"It's a long story. Not one I'm too proud of."

They stood clinging to each other, tears streaming down both their faces.

"I have all day. Start spilling, big brother." She smiled, wiping the tears from her cheeks. Beyond all hopes and dreams, she could never have imagined a better surprise.

"When I was seventeen, I was a smart-aleck teenager, and I got into a lot of trouble, including drugs. Mom and Dad sent me away to this place that was supposed to straighten me out. To make a long story short, I thought I had the world by the tail, and I ran away." Pete shook his head.

Essie could see how it must hurt Pete to recall his past, but she had to hear it — every little detail. "And you just kept going. I can't believe you never came back."

"The longer I stayed away, the harder it was to go back." He shrugged his shoulders and spread his hands. "I was a stupid teenager."

"You never got in touch with them." Essie couldn't imagine the heartbreak her parents went through. Did they really think he was dead, or why didn't they tell her? Did they think she would never find out?

"That's the one thing I regret more than anything. I should have at least let them know I was okay."

She saw tears rolling down his cheek.

"But you came to see Nana," she said, motioning to the picture.

"When I found out Mom and Dad had been killed, I came

to see Grams. It was shortly before she died." Another tear fell down his cheek.

"Where have you been all these years? What have you been doing?" She ached to know everything about his life.

"I was on the west coast, mostly. It was there I met a retired minister, and he and his wife took me in and gave me a different perspective on life. I got my GED, worked several jobs, and made some good investments."

"I don't understand why you didn't tell me," Essie said, flabbergasted.

"I didn't want to tarnish the Euller name. Our grandparents were highly esteemed and well-respected in this town. I made Grams promise not to tell." He held her at arm's length. "I would have eventually told you, honestly. I wanted to establish a better name for myself before the truth came out."

"But half of what I have should be yours. You can move in here with me," Essie said, a desperate tinge in her voice.

"No way! Besides, I have my own house in the making. I might as well tell you. I've bought the Sawyer place." He chuckled. "That was the reason I tore out of here when the fire started."

Her mouth flew open. "You can't live in that place. You're going to move in here with Jamie and me," she demanded.

"You won't know the place when I get through with it. The frame is structurally sound, and I'm going to completely gut the insides. I plan to start building in early spring. I should be in it before the summer is over."

She could see the excitement on his face when he talked about it. "So what about all the strange things that have been going on there. The lights, was that you?" Essie asked.

"No, probably kids partying. They won't do it anymore because I'm boarding up the windows. I just closed the deal a few weeks ago."

The deal! She burst out laughing. So that had been the deal she'd happened upon. She thought of what Claire had told her.

"Rumors are that you were sneaking around there with a seedy-looking character."

He laughed. "And that would be the realtor with his long hair. As for the sneaking, yes, I wanted to surprise you."

"I can't believe you're my brother." She threw her arms around him again. "If I had a choice out of the whole world, I would pick you."

"Why do you think I've been so protective of you? I wasn't going to let anything happen to my little sister."

Essie's heart melted at the words. "Just wait until Jamie finds out. Now, instead of Mr. Pete, you'll be Uncle Pete."

"And a very proud uncle, too. But now I need to go. I have some windows to board up."

"But I don't want you to go. I've just found you. We have almost thirty years to catch up on." She squeezed him tight.

He squeezed her back. "And we will, but I want to seal the place up before the same thing happens again." He stopped at the door and looked at Essie. "Maybe we should keep this to ourselves until we figure out a way to tell everyone."

"You want me to keep this to myself?" She gasped in awe. "I just found out I have a brother, and I can't tell anyone. I'll burst if I have to keep this inside me. I don't know if I can, but I'll try," she promised.

He grinned his Mr. Pete grin. "Just for a couple of days."

After Pete left, Essie couldn't calm herself. She paced back and forth, throwing her fists in the air. "Thank you, God, for my brother and for my son. I have everything I'll ever need in this world. Thank you, thank you, thank you."

At two in the afternoon, her doorbell rang. Her elation still high, she went to answer it, thinking it might be Pete. Her knees weakened when she saw Diana, the one person she least wanted to see, standing there.

As she was feeling very awkward, her emotions ran between disappointment and anger. Had she come to tell Essie to stay away from Lark? Well, she wouldn't have any problem there.

"Essie, I need to talk to you. Is it okay if I come in?" Diana asked cautiously.

Essie opened the door wider and motioned her in. "May I take your coat?" She forced herself to be polite.

"No, I won't be long. I'm moving today, and I have a lot to do."

"You're moving to a different place? Didn't you just move a couple of months ago?" For a brief moment, she imagined Diana moving in with Lark.

"Not to a different place. I'm moving out of town. My parents have just moved to Florida, and I've taken a job there so I can be near them."

The relief that overwhelmed Essie made her giddy. "Right about now, with all this snow, I wouldn't mind being in Florida." She embarrassed herself at the effort to make conversation.

"The reason I came by was because I wanted to talk to you about Lark. Somehow, I think I'm the cause of keeping you two apart."

Essie's eyes widened at the words. "Lark's a grown man. He's capable of deciding who he wants to see." She was uncomfortable with the conversation but couldn't turn away from it.

"I just wanted you to know there's never been anything romantic between us. The man is crazy about you."

Diana sounded sincere, but Essie still had doubts. She had to know the whole truth of what had been going on. "I don't think I believe that. I saw you kissing, and only yesterday, you were pretty cozy." Try as she might, she couldn't keep the suspicion out of her voice.

Diana laughed. "Let me explain about Lark and me. When my husband left me, I was devastated. Lark came to me and offered to save me from the wolves, so to speak. I was a real mess. I admit I had a small crush on him. He was handsome, charming, and very attentive, which was everything my husband was not. But he made it very clear to me from the very start that he was only there to support me. That kiss you were talking about at Uncle Ziggy's, right? That was the night Lark told me it was about time I stand on my own. I jokingly told him it was the longest relationship I'd ever had without a kiss. That's when he kissed me. As for yesterday, we were saying goodbye. I will always be grateful to him. He's a loyal friend, but I don't have romantic feelings for him, honestly."

"I appreciate you telling me this. I admit, I was jealous." Relief flooded through Essie so strongly that she thought she might tip over. She could barely believe the words she was hearing, but it all made sense now. Just when she thought her life couldn't get any better, here was this wonderful lady telling her that her fairy tale dream of so long ago was about to come true. *What a day!*

"I want nothing but the best for Lark. My pride has stood in the way long enough. I wanted people, and especially my husband, to think I was in a relationship. I realize now that it was selfish of me to ask Lark to go along with that. Being the person Lark is, he honored my wish." She reached out her hand to Essie. "I have to go now." She headed for the door, then turned. "Essie, Lark is a good man. I feel privileged to have known him, and I wish you two the best."

Essie's mind raced. That tiny bit of doubt about Lark had been erased with just a few words by this beautiful lady, who was moving to Florida and out of hers and Lark's life. The elation she felt couldn't be satisfied by a simple thank you.

"Is it okay if I give you a hug?" Essie asked.

Diana reached her arms out to Essie. "Thank you for understanding. Lark doesn't know I'm here, but I couldn't go without doing this. He's a very selfless man. You're lucky to have his love."

After Diana left, Essie didn't know what to do with herself. Trying to curb her emotions, she decided to go for a short walk. Going to the closet for her coat, she noticed the *Proud Mama* blouse Lark had given her for her birthday, which she'd never worn. Lovingly rubbing her hand down the front, she felt something in the small pocket. She pulled out a card with a small heart necklace fastened to it. On the back, Lark had written, *From my heart to yours.*

In that moment of ecstasy, she pictured God's giant hands opening up and pouring his blessings down on her.

She looked at her watch, then went to the mirror and fastened the necklace around her neck. Putting on her coat, she picked up her keys and purse and ran out the door. She knew exactly where she was going.

As she got to the school, the children were loading onto the buses. She hurried to Jamie's classroom. Lark stood at the chalkboard, his back to Essie, writing tomorrow's lesson as Joey and Jamie stood beside him. Essie caught Jamie's eyes, but before Jamie could say anything, she put her finger to her lips and tiptoed toward them.

"Is Mrs. Jordan really moving, Daddy?" Joey asked.

"Yes, she is. It's just the two of us now, bud."

Essie moved beside Lark and softly touched him on the arm. "And Jamie and me, makes four."

At the sound of her voice Lark turned slowly, his eyes expressing a deep love Essie knew was reflected in her own eyes. Her heart beating wildly, she reached her hand out to him. Seeing the confusion on his face as he slowly took her hand, she stepped closer and tipped her head upward, only inches from his face. "What," she said. "Can't a girl change her mind?"

Laying his hand on her cheek, he drew her into his arms and, looking tenderly into her eyes, answered, "Most definitely."

She fingered the small heart around her neck. "From my heart to yours," she said, showing him the necklace and grinning up at him.

The moment he kissed her, Essie knew it was no longer a fantasy. Her dream had come true at last.

Watching them closely, two happy little boys shared a hearty high-five.

ESSIE'S CREAMED CARROTS

Cut carrots into small sticks about one-and-one-half inches long. Put in pot and cover with water. Add chicken bouillon to taste and cook until not quite done. In a skillet, pour oil and sauté a whole onion, cut into thin rings. Add flour for thickening. Pour enough liquid from carrots into onions until of creamy consistency. Add carrots, put in a casserole, and bake at 325 degrees for about forty-five minutes or until it bubbles.

ABOUT THE AUTHOR

Audrey Dean grew up in Louisiana and is a long-term resident of Wisconsin. She has been writing poetry and prose most of her life, focusing on family-friendly fiction with influences from both her worlds. And Two Makes Four is her first contemporary romance novel.